RUBY TUESDAY

Wild Irish, book 2

MARI CARR

This story is dedicated to my devoted my Facebook friends. Your encouragement, support and shared laughter have meant more to me than you will ever know.

"I have learned you can **NEVER** go wrong with a book written by Mari Carr." ★ ★ ★ ★ ★ *Christine Redburn, Goodreads*

"I am **hooked** on this author!" ★ ★ ★ ★ ★ *Tammy Moody, Goodreads*

"When I finish a book with literally **a smile on my face**, it is a good sign." ★ ★ ★ ★ ★ *Christi Snow, Goodreads*

"As much as I enjoyed the first one, I liked this **even better**." ★ ★ ★ ★ ★ *Lucy Felthouse, Goodreads*

"Mari comes up with some **great characters**!" ★ ★ ★ ★ ★ *Irisdiana, Goodreads*

"Loved the sexual tension in this one, but **be warned**: reading this series cold make you hanker for an Irish beer." ★ ★ ★ ★ ★ *Sami, Goodreads*

Playlist

Fans of Spotify! Now you can access the Ruby Tuesday playlist.

And So It Goes by Billy Joel

Leave Me Alone by Helen Reddy

In Spite of Ourselves by John Prine and Iris DeMent

Champagne Supernova by Oasis

December 1963 by Jersey Boys

Beyond My Wildest Dreams by Little Mermaid Broadway cast

I Gotta Feeling by Black Eyed Peas

Forever by Chris Brown

And be sure to check out the Wild Irish "titles" playlist while you're there.

Come Monday – Jimmy Buffett

Ruby Tuesday – The Rolling Stones.

<u>Waiting for Wednesday</u> – Lisa Loeb and Nine Stories.
<u>Sweet Thursday</u> – Matt Costa
<u>Friday I'm in Love</u> – The Cure
<u>Saturday Night Special</u> – Lynard Skynard
<u>Any Given Sunday</u> – Sandpeople

Monday's Child

Monday's child is fair of face,
Tuesday's child is full of grace,
Wednesday's child is full of woe,
Thursday's child has far to go,
Friday's child is loving and giving,
Saturday's child works hard for a living,
But the child who is born on the Sabbath day,
Is bonny and blithe and good and gay.

~Traditional nursery rhyme

Chapter One

"Oh. My. God," Riley murmured behind her.

Teagan Collins struggled not to roll her eyes as she turned to see what had elicited such a response from her younger sister. Riley was the queen of sarcastic humor and no doubt she'd spotted someone who would now fall victim to her cutting wit. Typically it was a comment about the way someone dressed or styled their hair. She knew the rest of the family found Riley's little remarks funny, but sometimes she felt they were just plain mean.

"I'm late start—" She broke off mid-sentence when she saw her sister actually appeared to have gone pale. "What's wrong?"

Riley stuttered a few moments before she could speak. "It's…it's h-him."

Teagan turned around and glanced at the men drinking in the pub. Summer was Baltimore's peak tourism season—it was currently a Tuesday night in late fall. To say the crowd was sparse was putting it lightly. A few regulars sat at the bar, hanging out with her pop and her brother Tris, fighting rather loudly over the results of Sunday's football game. It was clearly going to be a long, hard winter as the Ravens didn't appear to be winning enough to suit this pack of rabid fans.

An older couple, Mr. and Mrs. Tibbs, occupied a table near the stage. She smiled when she saw them. They were quite possibly as close to groupies as she would ever get. She wasn't foolish enough to aspire to singing greatness. She knew achieving fame and fortune as a professional singer was as likely as winning the lottery. Besides, her love for music centered more on songwriting than performing, but she did appreciate the kind comments and encouragement the elderly couple gave her each week when she took the stage.

The only other two people in the place were strangers to her. She studied the two guys who sat in a corner booth, engrossed in what appeared to be a serious conversation. One was blond and somewhat handsome while the other had dark hair and an unattractively bushy beard. His face was in shadow, making it difficult to distinguish his features. She guessed they were both in their mid-twenties.

"Him who?" Teagan asked.

"Sky Mitchell," Riley whispered, her voice almost reverent.

"Who's Sky Mitchell?"

Her sister's gaze left the two men and traveled to

Teagan, wide with disbelief. "Are you freaking kidding me? Tell me you're joking."

"About what?"

"You honest to God don't know who Sky Mitchell is?" Riley asked, her voice laced with genuine amazement.

"Should I know who he is? Did you go to high school with him or something?" Teagan glanced back at the table and tried to decide if either of the men looked familiar. They didn't, although in all fairness, the lighting in the pub was dim and the dark-haired man had a baseball cap pulled down low over his face.

"High school!" Riley said. "Don't I wish! Sky is only the lead singer of the hottest rock group on the radio these days. Please God, tell me you've heard of The Universe."

Teagan nodded, her eyes narrowed. She'd have to live under a rock not to have heard of The Universe. "Of course I've heard of them. I just didn't know the name of their lead singer. Besides, that's not really my kind of music."

"Oh, that's right," Riley began. Teagan braced herself for the words she knew were coming next. "They sing songs that were written in this decade."

"There is nothing wrong with folk music, Riley. Nothing wrong with enjoying songs that have some deeper meaning than 'I wanna get laid'."

"You know, not all songs revolve around sex these days."

Teagan shrugged. "I wouldn't know since I can't

understand a word any of them is screaming—uh, sorry—singing."

"Sky's not like that. His voice is pure gold. And he is tee-totally hot."

Teagan looked back at the men, certain neither of them really fell into that category. "Which one is Sky?"

Riley groaned. "Holy shit. I honestly can't believe we carry around the same genes sometimes." Teagan silently agreed. "He's the one in the hat, wearing the fake beard."

"How can you tell he's Sky Mitchell? I can't even see that guy's face."

"I would know that hunka-hunka burnin' love anywhere," Riley joked.

"Aw jeez. Well, I've officially been in this conversation five minutes longer than I wanted to be. I'm going to go sing."

"In front of *him*?" Riley asked. For the first time in her life, Teagan thought her sister seemed to eye her with an air of respect.

"That's the general idea."

"You aren't nervous?"

"Why in the world would I be nervous? I sing in front of strangers practically every day."

"But that's Sky Mitchell," Riley pointed out.

"So you keep saying."

Riley took a step back and studied Teagan's appearance with obvious distaste. "Why don't you run upstairs and put on some makeup first? Maybe change out of your hippie garb. I've got a smoking-hot, red leather miniskirt that would—"

Teagan shook her head. "My outfit is fine. Why don't *you* go get dolled up for him? You're clearly interested."

Excitement sparked in Riley's eyes. "I can't believe I didn't think of that!" She turned toward the stairs that led to the family's apartment. "Holy hell. I almost offered Sky Mitchell to you. What the fuck was I thinking?"

"I have no idea," Teagan muttered, secretly amused Riley would actually think for one second she'd go after a rock star.

"Don't let him leave. I'll be back in a flash. And please, Teag, don't sing your usual shit. Sing something contemporary, upbeat—freaking *sexy*."

Teagan narrowed her eyes. "Gee, I don't think I know any songs like that."

Riley was too distracted to notice the smartass remark. "You're a songwriter, for chrissake. Make something up. Just don't let him leave this bar 'til I get back." With that, Riley disappeared and Teagan fought to regain her composure, her energy. Conversations with Riley tended to wear her out.

Her sister Keira had moved out over the summer to shack up with her handsome English professor, Will, leaving Teagan to share a bedroom with their younger sister. Despite the fact that her brother Killian was currently stationed in Iraq and her baby brother Sean had found his own apartment, there were still four Collins kids left at home. And sometimes she thought Riley should actually count as more than one sibling. Her sister was a handful on a good day.

She glanced at the two men in the corner again and panicked for a moment when the blond man rose to leave. Riley would seriously freak out if they were gone when she returned. The two men shook hands and she overheard Sky say he'd meet his friend back at the hotel later. The blond left and Sky leaned back for a moment. She watched him take in the room, his eyes only briefly brushing over her as she stood in the center of the room with her guitar. Then he opened a notebook and picked up a pen. She walked to the stage, wondering what he was writing.

Probably his memoirs. No doubt one of those VH1-style nightmare tales of the poor, pitiful rock star who's overcome drug abuse and endless orgies to go on to bigger and better things.

She struggled not to roll her eyes at the thought as she took her place on the stage and quickly tuned her guitar. She smiled at the patrons and sang a few of her favorites—songs by John Prine, Leonard Cohen and Nanci Griffith. As she sang, she kept one eye on Sky—who continued to write in his notebook, only glancing up occasionally—and one eye on the staircase to the apartment. Riley sure was taking her sweet time getting ready. Of course, knowing her sister, Riley had decided Sky Mitchell was worthy of what the family had jokingly dubbed the "Saturday Night Special". Riley spent hours primping prior to going out and partying until the wee hours every Saturday.

From the standards, Teagan moved on to some of her original material, singing four songs the patrons of the bar had heard often. She smiled when the regulars sang along during the chorus. She loved singing her own songs the best. The music never failed to move her.

She decided to end the set with a new song she'd just finished writing that morning. She was proud of the song, *Maybe Tomorrow*, and felt perhaps it was one of the best she'd ever written. At least it fit into Riley's request for an upbeat song. It had a fun, whimsical melody with playful words. As she began strumming the guitar, she felt herself floating away to what she thought of as her happy place. Every now and then, she'd simply lose herself in the music, in the sheer joy of singing and playing. She let her voice flow around the words and weave itself into the sounds coming from her beloved acoustic guitar. The guitar had been her mother's before she died and it was Teagan's most cherished possession.

As the song ended, she was surprised to realize most of the chatter in the bar had died down. Instead of the polite applause she was accustomed to, she received hearty cheers from the old guys at the bar and Mr. and Mrs. Tibbs had risen to their feet. She grinned and thanked them.

Putting her guitar down on the stand, she'd forgotten all about Sky Mitchell—until she stepped off the small stage and bumped into him at the foot of the stairs.

SKY WATCHED the colorful gypsy descend the two steps of the stage, not even aware of the fact he was crowding the small space at the bottom until she ran into him. She stumbled slightly and he quickly wrapped his arms around her waist to steady her. He was surprised to discover how small and shapely she was beneath her voluminous clothing. With her long, flowing skirt and baggy, loose-fitting top, he'd been unable to discern if she had any figure at all. To top it off, the blinding outfit was a kaleidoscope of color—purples, yellows, greens and blues all competing for dominance in the wildly patterned material, which made it tough to focus on anything at all.

Until her last song, he'd never made it past her crazy clothing to bother looking at her face. Now that she was literally right under his nose, he grinned like a lovesick fool at the wholesome visage glancing up at him. She had long, rich red hair, bright green eyes and honest-to-God freckles that covered nearly every square inch of her pale complexion. She wasn't beautiful, but she sure as hell was pretty, striking. He felt his cock stir and fought to bring the unruly thing under control before it embarrassed him. His jeans were too tight to allow him to hide even a mild hard-on.

"Excuse me." He made certain she'd found her balance before taking a step back. He studied her expression, waiting for the inevitable moment when she would recognize him. His disguise was a weak effort and there was no way it would fool this woman now that they were standing so close together.

"I'm sorry," she said. "I didn't see you standing there."

He counted to five in his head, surprised when the

usual fawning, "oh my God" reaction didn't come and an awkward silence fell between them.

"Um, I was quite impressed with your set, especially that last song," he said, aware he sounded a bit like a babbling idiot. What the fuck was going on with him? "You have a lovely voice."

"Thank you," she replied. "I have to confess I just finished writing that final song this morning."

"So you're a songwriter in addition to a performer?" His interest in her rose higher. He was hiding out in Baltimore, taking a long-needed hiatus from touring with his band and grappling to make a serious decision regarding his future. He'd started writing songs for his next album. An album he hoped to record solo, though he hadn't confessed that dream to too many people. In fact, he'd only just sprung the idea on his best friend, Rod, tonight. His friend had understood his need to try something new and Sky had appreciated his support.

"Actually I think it would be more accurate to say I'm a songwriter who performs occasionally."

"You sing well enough to have landed the gig here," he said, surprised someone with so much obvious talent would sell herself so short.

She laughed at his words and he grinned at the music in the soft sound. "It's my family's pub."

"Ah," he said. "I was wondering if you would join me for a drink. Just until your next set. I'd like to talk to you about your music." He wanted to buy that last song. He knew the moment he'd heard *Maybe Tomorrow* he'd found the title track for his album.

"Um, sure," she said and again he was shocked by her hesitance. It dawned on him that either she didn't know who he was or she didn't care. Both answers were so atypical he found himself uncertain how to react. "Let me just pop over to the bar to get a glass of water and I'll come right back. Can I get you something?"

He shook his head and gestured to the untouched beer on his table. "No thanks. I'm good."

He watched her walk across the room before returning to his booth. As he sat, he felt a welcome sense of optimism rising within him, a hopefulness that sadly had been lacking in his life lately. For the past decade, he'd eaten, slept and breathed nothing but The Universe, touring ten months out of the year, recording the other two and loving every single moment of it… for a while. Then nearly a year ago, he'd hit the wall. Burned out. He'd realized he had reached the point in his career where he needed a change. He'd gone as far as he could go with the band and he was dying for a new adventure, a bigger challenge, something different.

When he'd made quiet noises about going solo, the band's manager, Marty, claimed he was merely over-worked and undersexed and suggested he take a break. It was Marty who'd sent him to Baltimore to relax for a month. He'd set him up in the penthouse of a swanky hotel under an assumed name and told him to hide out —get drunk and laid—until The Universe's last sched-uled concert over Thanksgiving weekend. Unbe-knownst to Marty, Sky had been putting the time alone to better use than sex and alcohol. He was determined to put together an album's worth of solo songs.

He scratched at the itchy fake beard on his face and wished he could rip the damn thing off. He glanced out the large plate-glass window at the front of the pub and decided against it. The paparazzi—always relentless—had stepped up their pursuit of him since his breakup with Holly Gonzalez, supermodel extraordinaire, and he'd had to take some extreme measures lately in order to fly under their radar.

He closed his eyes wearily as Holly's plastic face flashed in his mind. Super *bitch* extraordinaire was more accurate. While he'd made a serious commitment to their relationship, it seemed Holly was only committed to the idea of fame and fortune. She was perfectly content with him when there were cameras flashing in their faces. It was when they were alone that things disintegrated. He'd finally read the writing on the wall when she suggested they invite cameras into their apartment and star in their own reality show. Their well-publicized breakup had only convinced him more that it was time for some serious changes.

"Hi again."

Sky looked up to find the singer standing by his table and realized he didn't even know her name. He rose quickly and gestured for her to join him. She placed her glass of water on the table and he nervously decided to take the plunge as they sat down. Perhaps she really didn't recognize him through his disguise, though he feared an introduction would generate the rabid fan response.

"I'm Sky Mitchell," he said.

She never skipped a beat as she replied, "Teagan

Collins. Nice to meet you." Her tone gave away nothing and again he was struck by the absurdity of the moment. He'd clearly spent too many years in the limelight if he didn't know how to hold a normal conversation with a new acquaintance.

"Teagan is an unusual name," he said, searching for some scrap to start the conversation since she obviously wasn't going to spend the standard twenty minutes gushing about how great he was and how much she loved his music.

What a relief.

She laughed lightly. "Yeah, well, I have Sunday to thank for that."

"Sunday?"

"My mother. She took the naming of her seven children very seriously."

Sky leaned back in the booth and grinned. "Seven children?"

"Yep." Teagan turned toward the bar. "In fact, if you take a look over there, you'll see two of my four brothers glaring at you from behind the counter."

"Ah, so they are. Should I be preparing for a 'pistols at dawn' challenge?" he joked.

Teagan shook her head, her smile growing wider. "I think you'll be okay so long as you stay on that side of the table. Tris and Ewan have learned a bit about restraint lately. My oldest sister, Keira, just recently moved in with her boyfriend."

"I think I'm beginning to understand your comment about the unusual names—Keira, Tris, Ewan."

"Actually, I have to confess all the names seem to fit. For instance, 'Teagan' means poet."

Sky nodded. "Very fitting for a songwriter."

"Your name is fairly unusual as well," she said.

"It's not my given name," he confessed.

"I didn't think it was. No doubt someone must have thought Sky was a terribly clever name for the lead singer of a band called The Universe."

"So you *do* know who I am."

"Of course," she said, and then she broke into peals of laughter. He was confused by her response until she added, "Actually, I had no idea until my sister, Riley, spotted you. I mean, I've heard of The Universe, but I have to admit it's not the type of music I usually listen to."

"Not a fan of popular music?" he asked, surprised. While her songs were definitely folksy, *Maybe Tomorrow* would be very easy to put a contemporary twist on by eliminating the acoustic guitar and adding more instruments.

"Not particularly. I prefer folk music. You know, songs where you can actually understand what the singer is saying." The moment the words left her lips, he watched her blush uncomfortably. "I'm sorry," she added quickly. "That was completely rude and I can't believe I said it."

He shrugged good-naturedly. "I'm not offended. I agree there are a lot of bands out there that rely on painfully loud music to drown out the fact that their lead singer can't sing or their words are utterly ridiculous. I hope you don't feel that way about The Universe's music."

She winced. "I was kind of hoping to avoid admitting the fact that I don't really know any of your songs. I mean, it's entirely probable that I've heard them on the radio and just didn't know it was The Universe."

Sky shook his head in disbelief. He wasn't so cocky as to believe everyone in the world knew the band's music, but it had been so long since he'd actually met someone who didn't, he wasn't sure how to react.

He watched Teagan glance at a spot behind him and he realized it was the third time she'd done so. He turned to see what she was looking at. All he saw was a staircase. "Are you waiting for someone?" he asked.

"My sister, Riley. She was excited when she realized you were here. She went upstairs to change her clothes."

He grinned. *That* was a response he could understand. "Is your sister as pretty as you?" he asked.

"She's much prettier. No freckles or bright red hair."

He was surprised by the sincerity of her response, as well as the lack of jealousy behind it.

"Oh Teagan, I had to tell you how much I loved that last song!"

Sky looked up to see an older woman standing by their table. He was struck by the fact that, once again, he was virtually invisible, as the woman never glanced his way.

"Thank you, Mrs. Tibbs."

"Bev wanted me to ask if you were still coming to teach the music class tomorrow."

"Of course I am," Teagan replied. "I wouldn't miss it for the world."

"Music class?" he asked.

Mrs. Tibbs looked at him briefly. "Teagan teaches music at my daughter Bev's preschool every Wednesday."

Sky pictured Teagan surrounded by small children. The thought *lucky kids* drifted through his mind as Mrs. Tibbs turned back to her. "I'm afraid my husband and I are leaving early tonight. His arthritis is bothering him again. Darn cold weather."

"Oh no. Tell him I hope he feels better soon. Good night," Teagan replied.

"Good night, dear." The older woman walked to the front door, where her husband waited to help her into her coat before they left together.

"Apparently Mrs. Tibbs doesn't listen to The Universe either. I can't begin to tell you what this evening has done for my ego," he joked.

Teagan laughed and he reveled in the genuineness of the sound. After years spent around women who giggled like schoolgirls or offered him husky laughter meant to sound sexy, he enjoyed the true humor behind Teagan's. His cock moved again and he forced himself to think of something other than what she would look like with that ridiculous skirt hitched up around her waist and him kneeling behind her.

"Believe me, Riley will more than make up for Mrs. Tibbs and me. Although I can't understand where she is. Even for her, this is an excessive amount of time spent primping. Maybe I should go check on her."

"Actually," Sky said, taking her hand quickly to keep her from rising. "I was hoping to talk to you about that last song you sang."

"*Maybe Tomorrow*?" she asked.

He nodded, and then decided to grab the bull by the horns. "It's a terrific song, Teagan. I'd like to record it."

"Record it?"

"I'm in Baltimore for the next month, working on songs I hope to record on my debut solo album." He wasn't sure why he felt compelled to tell her about his plans, but the moment the words flew from his lips, he knew his decision to break away from The Universe was finally made for good. No more waffling back and forth—starting tonight, his new direction was set.

"Solo album? You're leaving The Universe?"

"I'm been toying with the idea for months, but yes," he said more assuredly, "I'm leaving the band." He'd have to break the news to Marty soon, but the fact was his contract with The Universe was about to expire and in a few short weeks, he'd be a free agent. The record company had been hounding him to extend his contract but he'd managed to hedge, claiming personal problems as the holdup. It was the only time his breakup with Holly had come in handy.

"My song isn't for sale," Teagan said, and the optimistic feeling he'd been enjoying crashed and burned.

"What do you mean it's not for sale? You said yourself you're a songwriter. Isn't it your goal to sell songs?" he asked.

"Yes…no…I mean, I've never really thought about it."

"Never thought about it?"

"I don't write music to make money, Sky. I write songs to make people happy. To share them with my family and friends."

"What kind of Rainbow Brite philosophy is that?" Her lack of drive astounded. Didn't she know how far she could go with her talent?

"'Rainbow Brite philosophy'?" He could tell from her tone he'd pissed her off, but the woman needed a wake-up call. "You pompous ass. There's no reason to insult me. Hasn't anyone ever said no to you before?"

"No one with common sense. I'm offering you a chance to hear one of your songs on the radio, maybe see it hit the *Billboard* list. This could launch your career."

"I have a career," she said.

"Singing in your family's bar in front of a handful of old men. Teaching music to a bunch of kids one day a week. That's your idea of a career?" he asked, uncertain why he was reacting so harshly. For some inane reason, it suddenly felt as if the success of his solo career was inexplicably linked to Teagan's song. Besides, the woman was extremely talented and clearly oblivious to the fact.

"I suppose you think I should be an overly ambitious musician. One who hops on the fast track to fame and fortune with no regard for the quality of my songs, no concern for what junk I produce so long as it makes me rich and famous. Is that right? You know, there are some people out there who actually make music just for the sheer pleasure of it."

Sky took a deep breath, aware that his anger was merely fueling hers. This wasn't the way to negotiate a deal. He knew better than this.

"I'm sorry, Teagan. My reaction was out of line. I've been running on empty for over a year now and I had no right to take it out on you. I love your song. Seriously love it. You said yourself you write songs to make people happy. I'm offering you a much bigger platform to do just that."

She fell silent for a few moments and he could see his words had struck a chord. "Would you change it?" she asked.

He knew this was going to be a sticking point for her, but he refused to lie. He had a definite idea of the sound he wanted and it didn't include an acoustic guitar. "I would add more instruments, change the pacing a bit."

"Electric guitar instead of acoustic?"

"I play the electric guitar."

"You can't play an acoustic one?" she asked.

He sighed and prepared for round two of the battle they seemed destined to wage over her song. "Of course I can, but that's not part of my signature sound. I'm known for my abilities on an electric guitar."

"I don't know how you could make my song mesh with so much noise."

"I hardly consider the music produced from an

electric guitar 'noise'," he said, mustering as much patience as he could to keep his tone even.

"Darn it. I did it again. I'm sorry, Sky. I don't think your music is noise. I've never even heard your music. I just don't think you understand the concepts, the subtleties of folk music well enough to do *Maybe Tomorrow* justice. I would die if my song suddenly sounded like every other song on the radio. Filled with overdone guitar solos, digitally enhanced singing and that blasted repetitive drumbeat. People can't even dance properly to most of the music produced these days. They just bob in place."

"How old are you?" he asked, cursing the words the moment they flew from his lips.

"What's that got to do with anything?" Her eyes narrowed angrily but he couldn't resist finishing his thought. She'd insulted him and his music one time too many—all without even hearing him sing.

"Your ideas about music and dance seem more fitting for a woman in her eighties. Hell, my grandma is more hip about music than you."

"It doesn't have anything to do with being hip. It has to do with personal preferences. If you were educated in more types of music, you'd realize there are some really fine songs out there that don't require more to move you than a single instrument and a beautiful voice."

"You think I'm not educated in music?"

"I didn't say that."

"Yes," he insisted, "you did—and you meant it. For your information, gypsy, I've studied music extensively.

In fact, I'll bet I have a better grasp of the subject than you."

She sat up straighter and for a moment, he was finally graced with the shadowy shape of her breasts through her damn loose blouse. Fucking thing was at least two sizes too big in his opinion and he felt his cock stir once again at the sight. Despite her antiquated opinions on music, Teagan had triggered some serious arousal in him. Maybe Marty was right. He did need to get laid.

"Don't do that," she said, leaning closer.

"Do what?"

"Undress me with your eyes."

He grinned. "How about I do it with my hands?"

"Are you finished?" she asked dryly.

"I haven't even started but believe me, when I do, you'll know."

"Can we get back to the conversation at hand?"

"For now. Teagan Collins, I want your song."

"And as I said, Sky Mitchell or whatever your real name is, it's not for sale."

He laughed at her no-nonsense manner. He was enjoying himself, and her casual dismissal of his come-on dispelled his anger and brought out a playfulness he usually only showed to close friends and family.

"Well," he said, "it would appear there's only one way to solve our disagreement."

Chapter Two

"I challenge you to a singing contest," Sky said.

His voice was loud as he spoke and Teagan fought to hide her dismay when several heads around the bar popped up, including Pop's. There was nothing the regulars at the pub loved as much as a contest. She could see genuine interest dawning and no doubt several of the older gentlemen were holding their breath, waiting for her response and praying it would be yes. She imagined Pop's hand twitching with the temptation of reaching into his back pocket and pulling out his wallet for a wager.

Crap.

"And what on earth would you hope to prove with a contest?" she asked. She spoke so softly that two men at the bar stepped closer to the booth, confirming her suspicion that everyone was listening.

"You think I'm a puppet in the industry. A talentless clod with no knowledge of music."

"I never said that," she insisted.

"You insinuated it. Truth is," Sky paused and glanced toward the bar. She recognized the moment he realized they were being watched. He looked back at her with a smile that clearly demonstrated his awareness that he held the upper hand. His voice was even louder when he spoke again. "Truth is," he repeated, "you've insulted my reputation and I think you owe me the chance to prove myself."

Pop sauntered over with fake nonchalance and Teagan knew she was lost. "Is there a problem here, Ruby?"

Pop adored her red hair, dubbing her with his own pet nickname. She'd heard more than a few of the pub patrons jokingly remark to Pop that the redheaded mailman must have delivered a big package the day she was conceived.

"Nope, no problem," she said quickly, well aware she wouldn't be let off the hook so easily.

"I couldn't help but overhear this gentleman challenge you to a singing contest. Surely he knows there's no way he could ever out-sing my beautiful lassie."

"Mr. Collins, I'm afraid there's the issue of my pride at stake here," Sky insisted.

Teagan curled her hand into a fist, feeling the irresistible urge to punch someone for the first time in her life. The man was playing Pop like a pro. "It was a misunderstanding," she started, but Sky interrupted before she could continue.

"And one that could easily be settled with a simple, friendly contest. You gentlemen," he said, including the other patrons of the pub in their conversation, "could stand by as judges."

And with that last sentence, he sealed her fate.

"Well, I don't see any harm in letting the boy try his talent against yours, Ruby girl. You have the most beautiful voice in the world."

"I'm afraid that's not exactly the kind of contest I had in mind," Sky interjected. "It would be like comparing apples and oranges to try to determine which of us sings better. It's too subjective. Besides, I don't think your daughter was insulting my singing as much as she was accusing me of a lack of knowledge in the different genres of music."

Pop nodded and Teagan wondered if he had a clue what Sky was talking about. She was fairly certain his mind was trying to puzzle out how to get his contest and how much he was willing to wager. "What did you have in mind then, Sky?" Pop asked.

"Sky?" she asked incredulously. "Pop, you know who he is?"

"I'd have to live in a cave not to know who the lead singer of The Universe is, Ruby. I'm old, not dead."

Sky flashed a cocky smile and she groaned. So much for his bruised ego. Pop had just administered the cure.

"I really don't think there's any contest that could —" she began.

Again, Sky cut her off. "It would all be in good fun," he said quickly. "With a few harmless wagers involved to make it interesting, of course."

Sky's mention of a bet opened the floodgates and she watched several patrons walk over to join them.

"Well, a contest sounds like a fine time," Pop said, rubbing his hands together gleefully. "What do you say we set the stakes?"

Sky rose from the booth and followed Pop to a table in the center of the pub. Five of her father's cronies and both her brothers joined them and she was struck by the fact they looked like the United Nations entering into peace negotiations.

"There was this game I used to play with some friends of mine when we were kids at summer camp," Sky said. He turned and beckoned her over. She grudgingly crossed the room. Clearly she wasn't going to escape this night without participating in whatever foolishness Sky had in mind.

"What sort of game?" Pop asked.

"Someone picks a word, any word, and Teagan and I take turns singing famous songs that contain that word in the lyrics. The game is over when one of us can't think of another song."

"And this is supposed to prove what?" Teagan asked.

"You don't think much of my musical knowledge. I'm going to prove to you that I know a thing or two. Besides, it's the wager that's going to settle our true differences, not the contest."

"If you think I'm going to let you win my song in some stupid contest—"

Sky held up a hand to stop her. "I don't want the song anymore."

"You don't?" she asked, confused by his easy capitulation.

He shook his head. "Perhaps I should clarify. I don't *just* want that song. If I win, you agree to help me write *all* the songs for my new album."

Her mouth dropped open and she physically fought to close it again. The gleam in Pop's eyes told her he not only approved of the stakes, but she feared he was suddenly hoping she'd lose.

"Think of it, Ruby. The Universe singing your songs. Your words and music on the radio." Pop was beaming.

Sky grinned at her and she knew Pop had justified Sky's belief that she should be reaching for the gold and aspiring to greater heights than she was currently achieving.

"And if I win?" she asked.

"What do you want?" Sky wiggled his eyebrows suggestively as he spoke and she rolled her eyes.

"The Universe is doing a concert here in a few weeks, right?"

He nodded.

"I want your portion of the proceeds from the concert," she replied.

He frowned. "So money is important to you?"

"Not for me," she added. "I volunteer at a nursing home here in the city. It opens its doors to elderly people who can't afford proper care on their own. The roof is leaky and they're in serious need of some modern conveniences. If I win, you give the money you make on the concert to them."

Sky smiled. "I suppose you give music lessons to the old people as well? Another part of your career?"

She thought she should take offense at his words, but she could tell he wasn't insulting her. She thought for a moment he seemed impressed, perhaps even moved.

"Music can be wonderful medicine for the soul."

"I agree," he said.

Ewan moved forward. "What's to keep one of the singers from stalling too long? I mean, we could be here all night waiting for one or both of them to think of a song."

"Good point," Tris added. "There needs to be a time limit. Say, three minutes to come up with a song or you lose."

Sky quickly agreed and she nodded, anxious to be done with the whole thing. "How much of the song do we have to sing?" she asked.

"Let's say two lines of the lyrics and one of them has to include the word," Sky answered.

"Fine."

"Well, then," Pop said gleefully. "It looks like we have ourselves a contest, boys."

Teagan fought not to shake her head with disgust when the men began plopping their money down on the table—side wagers, Pop said, as they began arguing about odds.

"So all we need is a word," Sky said.

"That's easy," Pop replied. "The word is 'ruby'."

She smiled at her father while her heart began to

race. A simple contest was one thing. Given the fact she didn't possess a competitive bone in her body, she usually never cared what the outcome was one way or the other. This time, she cared *too* much. Her hands felt clammy and she was slightly lightheaded. The nursing home could really use the money from Sky's concert.

But more importantly, she didn't want to lose. Not to Sky. She couldn't explain why, but she felt that by losing to him, she'd be losing more than a few songs. Tonight could set in motion events that could change her whole life. Keira had accused her more than once of selling herself too short due to fear of the unknown, but she didn't agree with her older sister. There was nothing wrong with enjoying her life as it was. She was perfectly content and she figured if she was happy, why seek a change that might make her unhappy? Put all her hopes and dreams into achieving something that might never happen?

"Shall we?" Sky gestured toward the stage and she watched as Tris placed another stool next to hers. She picked up her guitar and felt a strange warmth at the feeling of sharing the stage with Sky. She always performed solo and she wasn't expecting the sense of camaraderie she felt when he joined her before their audience—such as it was. She shook her head to jar the silly thought loose. They were competitors, not partners. God, she really was overwrought.

"Ladies first," he whispered when she hesitated.

She cleared her throat and sang the chorus of Pop's favorite Stones song, *Ruby Tuesday*.

Sky shocked her by following up with one of her favorite songs by Tom Waits. Back and forth they sang, and each time she found herself impressed with the scope and variety of Sky's song choices. While she performed lyrics by Helen Reddy and Johnny Cash, Sky contributed songs by Ray Charles, The Killers, even Seals and Croft.

As he sang a snippet of *Ruby Baby* by the Beach Boys, she realized that throughout their competition she'd fallen more and more in love with his voice. He really could sing. They'd shared her guitar, taking turns with it, and she marveled at his ability—hell, his incredible talent—with the instrument. She'd been an ass and she'd been terribly, terribly wrong. Sky was the real deal and she wasn't looking forward to the humble pie she was going to have to eat at the end of this contest.

"Sixty seconds, Teagan," Ewan prodded from his seat at the front table. He'd served as timekeeper throughout and his reminder brought her back to the present. It was her turn and she'd wasted all her thinking time lusting over Sky's voice. She panicked when she realized she was also out of songs.

"Ten seconds," Ewan said and she could hear the pleading tone as her brother sent her silent encouragement.

Finally, she shrugged and admitted defeat. "I can't think of any more songs." She turned to Sky with an outstretched hand. "You win."

She expected him to gloat and was surprised when he simply stood quickly, took her hand and pulled her off the stage. She wondered about his sudden haste, especially when he leaned closer and whispered in her ear.

"Hide me."

"What?"

"Hide me. Quick. Please."

She reacted before she could think, grabbing his hand and dragging him down the short hallway off the bar to a small storage closet. He pulled her in behind him, shutting the door with surprising force.

"What's wrong?" she asked.

"A few cars pulled up on the street as I sang that last song. I'm fairly sure the paparazzi have descended."

"Paparazzi?"

He was saved from answering her question when Ewan opened the closet door and joined them in the tight space. "Given the odd tour you've requested from my sister, I'm assuming you spotted the cameramen."

"How many are there?" Sky asked.

"Too many," Ewan replied.

"Shit. Front and back of building?"

"As far as I can tell, just the front. I take it you don't want to be seen?" her brother asked.

"That would be an understatement. Have they seen *you*?" Sky asked Ewan.

"Why?" she and her brother asked in unison.

"I may need some help getting out of here, a decoy."

Teagan looked from Ewan to Sky and realized there was a slight resemblance. They were definitely the same build and shared similar coloring.

"Okay. What do you have in mind?" her brother asked, clearly ready to lend a hand.

Sky whipped his shirt off and handed it to Ewan. "Put this on."

Ewan complied, shedding his shirt quickly and laying it on the counter behind her. Teagan could see Sky's mind working over the puzzle of how he could escape. He studied her for a moment and she wondered what was going through his mind.

"Can you gather a few things without being seen? Like a scarf and a change of clothes for Teagan?" Sky asked.

Ewan only hesitated for a moment. "It might take me a few minutes. You two stay here. I'll see what I can do." With that, Ewan left.

"Change of clothes?"

Sky nodded absentmindedly and she could see he was disturbed by the sudden turn of events.

Strangely, she felt afraid. "The paparazzi are a bad thing?"

"More like an annoying thing. Sort of like a swarm of fucking giant bloodsucking mosquitoes. Pardon my language. I thought I'd escaped the bastards. They're supposed to be staking out my house in Palm Springs."

"So now they're stalking you here. Isn't this all pretty commonplace for you?"

He sighed heavily and she felt her heart twinge at the sound. "Yeah, I guess so."

He began to pull off the heavy fake beard he'd been sporting all night. As more and more of his face was revealed, Teagan felt all the breath leave her body.

His features, no longer obscured by the ugly disguise, were shockingly, stunningly handsome.

"Oh," she whispered when he pulled off the last piece.

He glanced up at the sound of her surprise and grinned. "Like what you see?" he asked in the cocky manner she was quickly becoming accustomed to.

"You do realize you sound like an asshole, right?"

"I'm a rock star, gypsy. It's all part of the package." His words were spoken lightly and she knew he was teasing.

"Yeah, well, knock it off. We've got bigger fish to fry. What are we supposed to do about the paparazzi?"

"I've been thinking about that and I have a plan. Sort of. As long as we act fast, I may be able to sneak out the back and make my way to the hotel without being spotted."

"I can drive you if you'd like." She figured she owed him the favor considering how rude she'd been in regards to his singing earlier.

"That could work," he said, though she could tell he was distracted by his own plans. "Take off your clothes."

"Ha," she laughed. "In your dreams." So much for her feelings of goodwill.

"Just your blouse and skirt, Teagan."

"Oh my God. You are relentless. How many times do I have to tell you—"

"I want to wear them."

She eyed him with serious concern and he laughed. "I'll put them on and sneak out the back door. Believe me, this won't be the first time I've worn something questionable to avoid those vultures."

"And I guess I'm supposed to flit around in my bra and panties while the *National Enquirer* photographer snaps away?"

"You can wear Ewan's shirt until he comes down with a change of clothes for you."

"Why don't you wait and wear those clothes?" she asked.

"Because I'm in a hurry and chances are good the paparazzi saw the backs of two people on the stage, you and me. Ewan can pretend he was me. I'm going to pretend I'm you."

"And who do I get to be? Barbra Streisand?"

Sky looked at her with amusement. "Do you know *any* famous singers from this decade?"

"Only one—Sky Mitchell, and he's a pain in the ass who's done nothing but remind me why I don't bother with contemporary musicians."

"I'm hoping your family can distract the paparazzi while I get out of here. I don't think you fully appreciate how relentless these cameramen are. I don't have much time before they surround the place. Ewan will be here soon with something for you to wear. Shit, if it's that big of a deal," he stepped over to the shelf behind her, "here's an apron too."

"I'm supposed to wear Ewan's shirt and an apron?"

"Gypsy, I'd prefer you hang out in this closet in nothing but your bra and panties until he gets back, but I suspect you have some sort of modesty to protect?"

"Well an apron's not going to hide much." She took

the apron and put it back on the shelf while Sky picked up Ewan's shirt.

"I'd like to make the move from the closet to the car as soon as Ewan gets back. He can put my clothes and ball cap on while I help him don the beard. Then he can go out into the pub for a drink while I make a beeline for the back door. I can hide there until it's safe for you to come out and drive me to the hotel. Hopefully they'll be distracted enough by Ewan that I can sneak out undetected."

"So you think the paparazzi will think they've made a mistake and leave once they see Ewan," she added.

"Yes. So long as none of those men out there give me away."

"Pop's friends would never do that. I have a sneaking suspicion you won their respect with that contest. Besides, they hate the press as a general rule—something about being old and Irish. I have no doubt they'll protect you to the death."

"I hope so. Fact remains, someone tipped them off about my whereabouts. There are very few people who know I'm in Maryland."

"I don't understand why you don't just walk out there and be done with it?" she asked, wondering at his extreme attempts to avoid discovery.

"I need this break, this privacy. If they figure out I'm in Baltimore, I may as well go home. I've spent a week enjoying the sheer peace and quiet. I want more. Besides, you aren't getting rid of me that easily. You lost the bet, remember? That means where I go, you go. How do you feel about paparazzi hounding you night and day while you try to write a dozen songs?"

"Turn off the lights."

"Why?" he asked.

"If I'm about to strip down to my skivvies, it won't be with you watching. We'll make the clothes swap in the dark."

"Spoilsport."

"Just make sure you stay on your side of the closet. I don't want to have to break any roaming fingers. I know you need those to play the guitar."

"You know you're going to fall into bed with me eventually. Why don't we save all the fuss and get down to business now?" he asked, his voice oozing with a deep sensuality she didn't want to acknowledge, despite the fact his words were obnoxious as hell.

"Gross. Are you going to turn off the lights or not?"

He gave her a cocky grin and reached back to flip the switch.

"Why don't I trust you?" she asked when the room was plunged into darkness.

"Maybe because you suspect I have this devil inside prodding me to give you two minutes before turning the lights back on."

"That's it. Forget it. I'm not about to——"

"But you should know right now the gentlemanly part of my conscience won't let me touch that light switch until you tell me to. Reach out."

"Why?"

"Because I want to give Ewan's shirt to you."

"Oh. Okay," she said as she felt around in front of

her for the proffered clothing. Their hands met and she snatched the material from his grip quickly. She heard the unmistakable sound of his zipper opening and she silently prayed neither of her brothers came back until they'd safely made the switch.

She hastily pulled her blouse over her head, struggling to put Ewan's shirt on in the dark. She wasn't sure when her hands started shaking. She tried to convince herself it was nerves and the chilly air in the small room. Her conscience refused to admit her sudden trembling could be based on any kind of misplaced desire for the arrogant rock star currently pushing all her buttons.

"Here," she said once she was decently covered. Ewan surpassed her in height the year he turned thirteen. His large shirt hung to nearly mid-thigh on her.

Their hands met in the dark and she handed him her blouse and skirt. "I feel ridiculous," she muttered.

"I'm the one about to plunge into cross-dressing and *you* feel ridiculous?" She could tell he was joking and she wondered what sort of life he led that it didn't bother him to wear women's clothing merely to escape a few cameras.

"You know, putting on a dress isn't going to hide the fact that you're a guy. Your face and hair will still show if anyone spots you."

"Which is why I asked Ewan for a scarf. Okay, I'm dressed," he said after a few moments. "You decent?"

"I guess so," she said, not sure she wanted him to see her in just her brother's T-shirt. She should have opted for the apron as well.

He turned on the lights and for a second she was blinded by the sudden brightness. Then she could see all too clearly—and she burst into laughter.

"Oh my God," she gasped. Sky rolled his eyes at her response, but she could tell by his smile he didn't mind her laughter.

Her giggles died when he took two steps toward her. "What are you doing?" she asked.

"You may find the image of me wearing *your* clothes funny, but seeing you in that T-shirt is seriously turning me on. Decided against the apron, eh?"

"I thought this would be decent enough."

His eyes darkened seductively and she realized she'd been terribly wrong in that assumption. She sucked in a deep breath, startled when his gaze landed on her lips. She licked them, her mouth suddenly dry.

"Do that again," he whispered.

"What?" she asked, her voice betraying her nervousness, her arousal.

"Lick your lips."

"This is silly," she protested, though her words were weak at best.

"I'm going to kiss you, Teagan."

"I don't kiss women," she joked, trying to regain control of the moment.

He grinned crookedly and she wondered if he could hear the unbearably loud pounding of her heart. He grasped her hand, dragging it along the front of her skirt, letting her feel the hardness of his cock buried beneath the flowing material. "Lucky for me I'm not a woman."

He bent forward, capturing her lips in a kiss. She was stunned by the gentleness, expecting him to simply step forward and capture, claim. He struck her as a man who took what he wanted, but this kiss felt more like a softly spoken request. He eased her into it, taking only what she was willing to give, slowly moving her down the path to more. His tongue prodded against her mouth and she parted her lips, welcoming him inside as she reached up to grip his shoulders. Her knees went weak and she found herself relying on his strength. His hands engulfed her waist and she moaned as his hard-on pushed against her stomach.

How long they kissed, she couldn't say, but she suspected Ewan had been clearing his throat for several moments before either of them realized he was in the closet.

"There are so many things wrong with what I'm seeing right now, I'm not sure what to react to first," he said as she and Sky turned to face him.

Sky laughed at the confused look on her brother's face as he took in their attire—or more correctly, her lack of attire. She knew instantly he'd made a major mistake as Ewan's eyes narrowed angrily. "I'm going to kick your ass, music boy."

Sky put his hands up in a gesture of peace when Ewan took a step toward him. "Not yet, you aren't. What's the story with the paparazzi? Did they see you?"

Ewan seemed as confused by Sky's response as she was. What did he mean by "not yet"?

"They're still here and they've surrounded the

place. Quite a few have set up shop in the back," her brother replied slowly.

"Fuck, we were too slow. Are they inside the pub?" Sky asked.

"No, Pop told them you weren't here and there wasn't room in the pub for all their damn equipment. He gave them the boot. Told them if they wanted to make asses of themselves, they could do it outside."

"So they've basically still got a bird's-eye view of the pub through that plate-glass window," Sky said, his words a statement rather than a question.

"We can close the blinds," she suggested. "That would make it hard for them to see anything at all."

"No," Sky said, rejecting the idea immediately. "That would just make them suspicious, confirm their belief that I'm here."

"They know you're here. I'm not sure what this costume change is going to prove," Ewan pointed out.

"I was hoping to make a dash out the back door, but it looks like that plan is shot to hell." Sky turned and looked at her. "Hey, that staircase in the pub. Where does it lead?"

She studied his face and realized he was already hatching a new plan. The man was amazing at subterfuge and escape tactics. "My family's apartment. But the only other exit once you get up there is a fire escape that leads to the back alley. According to Ewan, the cameramen are there as well now."

"Do you think your pop would mind if I hid out upstairs for a while? I could lie low until the paparazzi give up and then call Marty, my manager. See if he can arrange discreet transportation through the hotel. There's a secure entrance there and so far no one has figured out I'm staying in Baltimore for sure."

"I think Pop would be okay with that," she answered.

"Why are we even bothering with this?" Ewan interjected. "The jig is up. They know you're here."

"No, Ewan, they don't know I'm here. They only suspect I am. Besides, need I remind you that I won the bet? That means Teagan and I are going to start writing songs for my next album. I'd prefer if we were able to do that in peace without having a bunch of cameras dogging our every move. If we can convince them it was you they saw, they'll think they've gotten a false report and split. I've got a friend I can call once I make it up to your apartment who can help me convince them they've made a mistake."

"So what's the new plan?" her brother asked. Teagan was surprised by his easy capitulation. It was clear Ewan still wanted to exact a bit of his annoying brotherly retribution on Sky for kissing her, so she couldn't understand his sudden willingness to go out of his way to help the man.

"I want you and Tris to distract the paparazzi—maybe get into a bit of a fight—while I walk upstairs. I don't think anyone will think much of a woman leaving the room during a brawl, if they even see me at all. Teagan, do you think you could recruit some help from your pop and his friends?"

"I'm sure I could. What do you want us to do?"

"I need the men to position themselves around the

fight in such a way that I can walk along that back wall to the stairs undetected from the street."

She nodded. His plan was a good one and surprisingly well thought out, considering he was planning on the fly. "That's no problem."

"Here," Ewan said, thrusting a pair of jeans at her. "Put these on."

She dressed while Ewan donned Sky's cap and stood still as Sky carefully applied the beard to his face.

"It's not ideal," Sky said when he completed the makeover. "But at least there's enough stickiness left to the glue to hold the thing in place. Just don't get too overzealous in the fight or the damn beard will fall off."

"I can handle my part," Ewan growled and Teagan feared this pretend fight with Tris would just be a warm-up for the real thing when they all got up to the apartment.

"Why don't you head out to the pub and let your pop and Tris in on the plan?" Sky suggested to Ewan.

"Come on, Teagan." Ewan tried to capture her hand and she knew hell would freeze over before her brother left her in the closet alone with Sky again. She started to follow, but Sky—foolish man—stopped her before she reached the door.

"Thanks for the clothes," he said with a charming grin.

She returned the smile. "I think I'm going to have to reevaluate my wardrobe choices. It sucks that my clothes are big enough to fit you and I'm seriously annoyed by the fact they look better on you than me."

Sky laughed and leaned forward to whisper in her

ear, his tone teasing and light, "Nothing would look better on me than you."

Teagan was thankful he'd spoken it too softly for Ewan's ears. She shook her head and rolled her eyes. "Rock stars," she murmured with a giggle before leaving the closet and heading back to the pub.

Chapter Three

Sky made his way up the stairs to the apartment above the pub. He could hear the scuffling noises of Tris and Ewan's pretend fight going on below, the patrons of the bar cheering them on. He grinned at how real the brawl had looked and determined the Collins brothers were no strangers to kicking each other's asses. Food for thought, since he'd certainly raised Ewan's ire in the closet. He mentally shrugged. The situation probably had looked bad from a brother's standpoint. He'd taken Teagan's clothes, leaving her in nothing but a T-shirt, and had been kissing her as though his life depended on it. The thought of her lips against his, her body pressed close…he shook his head to jar the memory loose. She was just a woman. He'd kissed thousands of them. No big deal.

So why did kissing Teagan Collins feel different?

"Fuck," he muttered to himself. "I don't have time for this." As he'd cut through the pub, he'd avoided looking directly out the window toward the paparazzi, but he felt quite certain no one had seen him or the cry would have been sent up. As far as he could tell, the press was enjoying the show the Collins men were putting on too much to notice the drag queen in the back.

He pulled his cell phone out of one of the deep pockets in Teagan's skirt. He'd tucked it in there earlier and he chuckled as he looked down at himself in her flowing, colorful garments. He felt like a damn fool. He hit speed dial as soon as he entered the apartment, shrugging the loose blouse over his head at the same time.

"Natalie," he said, when his friend answered the phone.

"Mitch, you asshole. Where the hell have you been? Palm Springs sucks without you."

"You don't miss me, babe. Just my bar and my pool and my mansion," he teased.

"That hurts, man. I swear to God I thought you knew me better than that."

"Oh sweet Nat, I know you far too well."

They both laughed as she conceded his point.

"I need a favor," he said.

"Anything."

One of the things he liked best about Natalie Miller was her unwavering friendship. She and Rod were the only remaining links he had to his younger days, to the days before he was Sky Mitchell, rock star. They'd been his friends in high school, back when he was just plain old Mitch Adams. Since then, their lives had taken them in different directions but their friendship had never wavered, never died. Rod had gone into real estate, Natalie into photography, and he'd struck it big on the stage.

"I need to lay down a false trail."

"Goddamn vultures. Found you again, eh?" Natalie asked. Her distaste for the paparazzi, if not stronger, certainly seemed to match his level of abhorrence.

"Yep."

"I'm on it. I've got some great shots from that long weekend you, Rod and I took in Cancun that I haven't shown anybody. I'll let a couple of you walking on the beach slip to the right people. Fucking idiots will run up a hell of a travel bill breaking their necks to get to Mexico." She laughed and Sky grinned at her deviousness.

Over the years, they'd started tricking the press as a means of escape for Sky. Natalie took pictures of him everywhere they went together, but never published them. Whenever he needed a break, she simply slid a few shots to the paparazzi under an assumed name, insinuating that she'd just taken them. She always got a nice chunk of change from the deal and Sky usually found some peace and quiet as the press traveled to whatever location she gave. She claimed the entire portfolio was her retirement plan. Once Sky gave her the go-ahead, she was going to publish a photo biography of him and, as she said, "sit back and roll in the dough." Until then, she had her own little studio and seemed content in her job, taking photos for weddings and other special occasions.

Sky secretly hoped he maintained enough popularity to make Natalie's dream come true for her someday. She'd been a genuine friend, through thick and thin, never once betraying him in hopes of a quick buck. She deserved a bit of easy street.

"So are you still at that swanky hotel in Baltimore?" she asked.

"I'm in Baltimore, but not at the hotel."

"Oh?" she asked, the question dripping with curiosity.

"You wouldn't believe where I was if I told you," he teased, dangling the truth in front of her.

"Tell me," she demanded.

"I'm in an apartment above an Irish pub dressed in the hippie skirt of a woman I just kissed in a storage closet."

"Shut up!"

"I'm serious," he said with a laugh. "I was going stir-crazy in that hotel even with Rod, so we decided to go out for a bite to eat."

"I thought Rod was leaving tonight on the red-eye," Natalie said.

"He is. He went back to the hotel to pack and rest up for a while. I decided to hang around."

"Is Rod feeling better? He had a pretty nasty cold when he left here."

Sky sighed. "I told him to go to the doctor when he gets home. Poor guy slept the whole time he was here and he still doesn't look good. He says it's allergies."

"I'll nag him when he gets back."

Sky grinned. Natalie was the supreme champion nagger.

"So you stayed behind at the bar? Alone?" she asked. He could tell from her tone she disapproved of him taking such a chance.

"The atmosphere was nice in the pub and I thought I might be able to pound out a few more lines of the song I've been working on."

"I take it the decision to hang around was a wrong one."

Sky considered her comment. Truth of the matter was, staying behind was probably one of the smartest things he'd ever done. Teagan was an unexpected treasure. He wasn't quite sure what the heck to do about her yet, but he fully intended to latch on to her talent for songwriting and possibly to any body part she'd let him touch. He hadn't been interested in or attracted to another woman since the Holly fiasco. Teagan had reignited his libido and her continued denial of his pursuit just spurred him on. God, he loved a challenge.

"Not necessarily," he said.

"Well, hell. It's the hippie, isn't it?"

"She's a songwriter. I challenged her to a contest and won. She now has to spend the next few weeks helping me write the songs for my solo album."

"Mmm hmm," Natalie hummed, her suspicion of the truth behind his reluctance to leave resonating in the sound. "She wouldn't also happen to be spending these next few weeks warming your bed, would she?"

Sky hoped so, but to hear Natalie word it so callously left him feeling a bit dirty inside. He hadn't seriously dated a woman since Holly, instead drifting from faceless woman to faceless woman. He hadn't exactly been promiscuous and he figured he wasn't a typical rock star in that regard. He didn't carve notches in his bedpost or keep a list for the day when he could write a tell-all about his wild years as a sex maniac. He just hadn't bothered to get to know any of the women he'd dated recently. He was looking for some good times at the moment, in and out of the bedroom, and as long as a woman didn't mind his lack of desire for a commitment, he was good. Once the talk turned to relationship, he hit the road.

"Wait a minute," Natalie said, her voice rising. "Back up the bus. Did you say solo album?"

"I've definitely decided to leave The Universe," he confirmed. "I haven't told anyone except you and Teagan yet, so let's keep that on the DL."

"Teagan, huh? Pretty name. Okay, mum's the word. So what's the plan for tonight?" Natalie asked.

He looked around at the Collins' apartment, taking in his surroundings for the first time. The living room was surprisingly spacious and he realized the family must inhabit the entire second floor. A staircase leading to the floor above insinuated they owned the entire building. "I'm not sure," he admitted. "Even if you sneak the photos to your contact tonight, I don't think the assholes down on the street will get the word right away. I may have to lie low here for a while, and then try to sneak back to the hotel. I'll call Marty later and see if he can hook me up with a ride."

"Is Marty in Baltimore?" Natalie asked.

"No, he's coming down next week to get things rolling for the Thanksgiving concert. Until then, I'm on my own." Sky heard footsteps on the stairs. "Hey listen, I gotta go. Do you mind calling Rod and letting him know I won't be able to see him off? Explain what happened."

"No problem. Behave yourself, Mitch."

He grinned at her usual comment. "You too, Nat."

"And be careful, you freak. A *hippie*," he heard her murmur as she clicked off. Natalie never said goodbye. It was a strange quirk of her character he found annoying and endearing at the same time.

As he turned, Tris, Ewan and Teagan emerged from below. Tris had a split lip and Ewan was sporting a large bruise on his forehead. Sky noted that—mercifully—the fake beard had remained in place. Teagan looked around the room and he could see she was confused.

"Problem?" he asked.

"Where's Riley?" she asked, concern written on her face. He noticed her brothers took the unexpected absence of their sister in stride.

"Who the hell knows? That girl comes and goes whenever the fuck she pleases," Tris grumbled, clearly annoyed by his inability to control this younger, wilder sibling Sky had yet to meet.

He watched as the three of them moved toward the kitchen area—separated from the living room by a wide, long bar—and worked as a team to wash away the blood and grab some ice packs. He marveled at their silent, well-rehearsed collaboration and wondered if perhaps his parents hadn't planned their family well. He wasn't exactly a stranger to large families as he was the middle child of three, but his eldest brother was six years older and his baby sister was four years younger. Fights were few and far between in his childhood home, while he thought they seemed to be rather common-place amongst the Collins kids, who all looked to be about the same age. In fact, as he watched them work, he was struggling to figure out who was the oldest.

"Okay," Teagan said at last as she blotted at a bit of blood that had dripped onto Tristan's shirt. "If you take that off now, I can soak it and I don't think it will stain."

Tris removed his shirt, surrendering it to his sister, and again Sky was struck by the family's closeness. Modesty didn't seem to exist either.

"I want to thank you all for helping me dodge the photographers down there. I've called a friend and I'm pretty sure the paparazzi will start to leave soon. We're laying down a false trail. Once the coast is clear, I'll take off," Sky said.

"Actually," Ewan added, "I think you should plan on spending the night here. There's an extra bed in my room you can bunk in."

Sky watched Teagan's eyes widen with surprise at her brother's offer and he chuckled. "Not planning to smother me in my sleep, are you?" he joked.

"Why would he do that?" Tris asked suspiciously.

"No reason," Ewan added quickly and Sky realized the man didn't intend to tell his brother about catching him kissing their sister in the closet. "Sky pointed out downstairs that he and Teagan are going to be working together on writing songs. I think they should do that writing here, rather than in a hotel room." Ewan emphasized the word *hotel* and Sky watched the light go on in Tristan's head.

"Oh yeah," Tris agreed. "You should definitely write here."

Sky looked around the apartment, thrilled by the invite. He'd been bored to tears cooped up in the hotel suite. He had a feeling life at the Collins' place would never be dull. Still, the devil in him prodded. "Oh, I could never inconvenience your family that way. Besides, Teagan and I would need a quiet, private place to work our magic. The hotel would be ideal for that."

He fought not to laugh as Ewan's face flushed at the word *magic*. Tris actually appeared to have swallowed his tongue, coughing uneasily.

"Sky," Teagan said, her eyes narrowed. "My brothers just went out of their way to help you tonight. Don't you think you should play nice?"

He grinned. "I'd love to stay here and I appreciate the offer of a bed. Are you sure your pop won't mind?"

Tris shook his head, his voice betraying his annoyance as he spoke. "Oh no, believe me, Pop will have no problem with the arrangement. He's downstairs all but passing out cigars to his cronies and bragging about his little girl writing songs for The Universe. I'd be surprised if you didn't get breakfast in bed."

"You mean that wasn't part of the deal anyway?" he joked, laughing when Teagan's eyes nearly rolled all the way back into her head.

"Can you ever be serious?" she asked, exasperated.

He walked over to her, wrapping his arm loosely around her shoulder, enjoying the ever-darkening looks from her brothers. "I'm a rock star, gypsy. I don't think breakfast in bed is too much to ask."

Teagan surprised him by moving forward rather than away. He'd expected her to shake off his arm, so when her own wrapped around his back, touching his bare skin, he fought to deny the sudden pounding of his heart. Women touched him all the time, so why was he reacting like a fucking teenager?

"You're standing here without a shirt and in my skirt. You look more like a half-dressed RuPaul than a rock star. If anyone should be getting breakfast in bed, it should be me for having to put up with you for the next few weeks."

He pulled her closer, ignoring her brothers, as he fought to retain what little bit of cocky Sky he could cling to. "Ooh, I do like the idea of us being stuck together," he murmured.

Out of the corner of his eye, he saw Tris and Ewan both take a step forward, but Teagan's reaction halted them in their tracks.

She reached up and grabbed his ear, twisting so hard tears sprung to his eyes.

"I'm only going to say this to you one time, rock star, so listen up. The only music you and I will be making is going to be on the page. If you don't knock off the sexual innuendoes, you won't have to worry about Ewan smothering you in your sleep because that's something you'll beg for after I cut off that protruding part of your body you call a brain. Got it?"

He gripped her wrist and fought to loosen her death grip on his earlobe. Growing up with rough brothers had obviously trained this woman well. She was as tenacious as a Rottweiler. The idea of what she was doing to his ear should have pissed him off, but he was even more aroused now than he'd been all night. She was a wildcat dressed up in "peace and love" hippie garb. Jesus, she was awesome.

"Got it," he said, relieved when she released him.

"Good," she said, turning toward a hallway that led away from the living room. "I'm going to bed. Night."

"Night," Ewan and Tris grumbled in unison.

For a moment, Sky expected both brothers to pounce on him and he regretted poking fun at them earlier. He was shocked when Ewan put a commiserating hand on his shoulder. "Fucking ear twist is deadly," he said. "Come on. I'll show you where my room is. I've got a pair of sweatpants you can sleep in."

Sky smiled appreciatively. Yep, he thought as he followed Ewan, he was definitely going to like it here.

TEAGAN WAS startled awake by a loud noise next to her bed, followed by some colorful cussing.

Riley was home.

She glanced at the clock, surprised to discover it was nearly dawn. "Where have you been all night?" she asked sleepily.

Riley turned around. "Sorry. Did I wake you?"

"You knocked over a chair and yelled 'Shit'. What do you think?"

"Long night," Riley replied wearily. "The tramp dumped Aaron."

Aaron Young and Riley had been best friends practically from the cradle.

"So what? You hated the tramp."

Riley sighed and sank down on her bed. "Aaron is unhappy. No, scratch that, he's miserable. I think in his fucked-up head, she was the woman he was going to marry. He called earlier from his house, drunk as a skunk."

"Aaron was drunk?" Aaron never drank. That was Riley's role in their friendship. She partied 'til she dropped and Aaron carried her home.

"I know," Riley said. "It freaked me out, so I went over and tried to cheer him up."

"I didn't see you leave," Teagan said.

"Took the fire escape to the back alley."

"Ah." The fire escape was Riley's main exit from the apartment. Teagan assumed it was because her sister was always moving in fast forward. Stopping to answer questions was enough to piss Riley off. God forbid she take time enough to descend a flight of stairs to the pub's front door.

Then Teagan smiled, trying to imagine Riley cheering anyone up. *Riling* someone up, Teagan could comprehend, indeed would expect of her sister. There was no one else she'd want at her back in a fight more than Riley—but putting a smile on another person's face? Mary Sunshine, her sister would never be. "Did it work?" she asked.

"I guess so. We just sort of talked until he passed out. I was too tired to drive home, so I dozed on his couch for a couple hours."

"Well, you missed some excitement here," Teagan said.

"Oh my God, that's right! Sky Mitchell! I can't believe I forgot about that. Don't tell me. He listened to one of your *Blowin' in the Wind* shit songs and hit the road."

"I thought you liked my singing," Teagan said, unfazed by Riley's comments. Her sister's continual insults about her folk songs had become an integral part of the fabric of their relationship.

"I love your freaking voice. You know that. You just waste it on stupid songs."

"Well, for your information, Sky did *not* leave after one song. He listened to the whole set and then invited me to join him at his table."

"Shut the fuck up!" Riley yelled, suddenly wide awake. She rushed across the room and jumped beside her on the bed so hard, Teagan nearly bounced off. "No way."

"Way." Teagan laughed.

"You lucky bitch. Tell me every gory detail. Don't leave out a thing."

"He heard me sing *Maybe Tomorrow* and he wanted to buy it. Record it on his next album."

"I told you that song was awesome," Riley interjected. "Holy shit. Your song's gonna be on the radio!

Hell, it could be nominated for Song of the Year. You could be invited to the MTV Awards! Can I walk down the red carpet with you?"

"Getting a little ahead of yourself, aren't you?" Teagan grinned at Riley's enthusiasm. Her sister's mind always raced at a speed most mortal humans could never achieve.

"Not at all. Everything Sky touches turns to gold. I swear this guy is Midas incarnate."

"Yeah, well, I turned his offer down."

Riley sat frozen for several seconds and Teagan could see she'd shocked her outspoken sister into speechlessness. "Tell me you're kidding," she said at last, her voice far too quiet. Teagan figured she'd better tell the rest of the story fast before Riley's head blew off her shoulders.

She quickly related the details of the contest, the arrival of the paparazzi, the storage closet—omitting the bit about the kiss—and ended the story by informing her sister that Sky Mitchell was sleeping in their brother's room across the hall.

Without a word, Riley rose from the bed and tiptoed over to Ewan's room. Teagan listened as her sister slowly opened the door. She imagined Riley peeking inside and screaming silently when she spotted her favorite musician snug as a bug in Sean's old bed.

When she returned to the room, she was eyeing Teagan with an expression that left her uneasy. "You're going to be writing songs with Sky Mitchell for weeks," Riley said, her voice far too even and controlled.

Teagan nodded in agreement, wondering what was going on inside her sister's mind.

"You should totally sleep with him."

"What?" Teagan asked.

"I'm serious." Her sister's face proved that she was, even though her words were utterly preposterous, even for Riley. "You have the opportunity to have sex with Sky Mitchell. Do *not* blow this."

"Have you considered the fact that I might not want to sleep with him? He's a cocky, arrogant asshole." Even as she spoke the words, Teagan knew they were false. She suspected he adopted that persona as a means of protecting himself and his flirting was little more than a part he was playing. People expected rock stars to be highly sexed creatures, so Sky gave them their money's worth. Besides, most of his sexual come-ons had merely been jokes, harmless teasing. She liked the part of him that tried so hard to make her laugh.

"Teagan," Riley said, placing her hands on her hips. Teagan settled in for the twisted lecture she was sure was about to follow. "You aren't exactly the most experienced woman in the world when it comes to sex. I mean, do you need two hands to count how many lovers you've had?"

Teagan narrowed her eyes, refusing to answer.

Riley continued. "Your silence proves that you don't. Besides, I'm your sister, I know exactly how many guys you've slept with and who they were." Riley shook her head sympathetically. "You poor girl. It's a pitiful list, you know."

She started to refute her sister's words, but she held on to the secret truth. Her sister believed the lies Teagan had perpetuated and she was happy to let them remain in place.

Fact was, she'd never slept with anyone. She'd long ago accepted the fact that most guys found her a bit quirky, a bit strange. Her outdated fashion style, antiquated taste in music, old-fashioned values and, well, pretty much everything else, set her apart. She wouldn't sleep with someone who couldn't accept her as she was and so far, that simply hadn't happened. Of course, that wasn't to say she hadn't fooled around, hence Riley's confusion.

"You have a chance to gain some real experience in the bedroom. I can't even begin to imagine what tricks Sky Mitchell must have up his sleeve as a lover. I bet he could fuck curls into that straight red hair of yours. Besides, this is something you can tell your children, your grandchildren."

"I'm going to tell my grandchildren that I had sex with Sky Mitchell?"

"Think about it, Teag. If Mom had pulled us aside and confessed to fucking Elvis before marrying Pop, you would have been impressed. Admit it." Riley said the words with such assurance, Teagan couldn't do anything but laugh. Her sister's warped vision of the world never failed to amuse her.

"I've never really thought of that, but I guess some small part of me might have thought that was cool. Maybe." Actually, Teagan thought she would have been more impressed to know for sure that her mother had never slept with any man except her father, the love of her life. Sadly, her mother had died when Teagan was sixteen and she had never had a chance to ask her mother the questions that burned in the back of her adult mind. Had her mother waited until after marriage? Had she regretted waiting?

"So you'll do it?" Riley asked.

"Do what?"

"Seduce Sky," Riley said impatiently. "Haven't you been listening?"

"I've listened and I've heard. I'll think about it, Riley."

"Don't think. Do."

Teagan smiled and lay back down on her bed. "It's too early to do anything right now. Do you mind if I sleep a few more hours before jumping Sky Mitchell's bones? If he's as wonderful as you seem to think, I'll need my rest."

Riley laughed, clearly appeased. "Sleep sounds good."

Her sister crawled into bed and Teagan shook her head in amazement as Riley drifted off to sleep instantly. It was an incredible talent her sister possessed and she was terribly jealous of the other woman's ability to fall asleep within seconds of laying her head on the pillow. Teagan, on the other hand, couldn't settle down to rest as her mind replayed Riley's words.

As he repeatedly liked to point out, Sky was a rock star. No doubt women fell into his bed like coins in a wishing well. There was no way she'd allow herself to become just another nameless face on his list of sexual conquests.

Was there?

For the first time in her life, she felt the principles she'd tried to live by wavering. She was tempted in ways she'd never faced and she wasn't sure she'd have the strength to continue to refuse Sky's advances. Truth of the matter was, her somewhat old-fashioned ideals had never been tested because she'd never met a man she wanted to sleep with. Until Sky. He was attractive, funny, talented and…shit. She sighed heavily. If he was a normal stranger off the street and they'd met in some ordinary way, she would definitely have said yes to a date with him. And she would have come upstairs after that first date full of anticipation and hope for a second.

But he wasn't normal. He was Sky Mitchell. And she was screwed.

Chapter Four

Teagan returned home from the preschool the next day feeling apprehensive, nervous. She'd snuck out of the apartment this morning like a thief as she'd tiptoed down the hallway and out the door far too early. She'd had to kill nearly an hour at a local coffee shop before the preschool even opened. Her restlessness in the face of Riley's bizarre sex lecture had left her out of sorts and confused and she'd run away rather than try to face Sky.

Now she'd had too much time to think about it all and she was on the verge of a serious panic attack. Or at least that's what she assumed this was. She was usually the queen of calm.

Shit. She never lost control of herself like this, but the thought of facing Sky while images of red-hot sex flashed through her mind seemed impossible. Sky would be able to sniff her arousal from a mile away. Her damn sister had pushed her onto the figurative ledge and she was definitely considering a jump—one that would either lead to nonstop masturbation or Sky's bed. Her heart raced as she climbed the stairs, her sweaty palms slick on the railing.

Laughter greeted her and she smiled despite her jangled nerves when she spotted Pop and Sky sitting at the counter eating Dagwood-style sandwiches.

"Hungry?" she asked as both men dug into the subs with enthusiasm. Riley's head popped up behind them.

"Where the fuck have you been?" her sister asked.

"Riley Collins," Pop chastised. "You will curb that filthy language or I will get out the soap."

"Jesus, Pop. I'm twenty-two years old. You can't wash my mouth out with soap."

"Riley," Pop said and Teagan watched her sister nearly bite her tongue off to obey. Pop was the only person left in the world who managed to retain a small bit of control over her sister.

"Welcome home," Sky said. "I was about to send out the troops to look for you."

"It's Wednesday. Music class at the preschool." She fought to keep her voice from betraying her anxiety and was proud of her efforts.

"So I recall."

Pop entered the conversation. "You should have called in sick, Ruby. You and Sky have a lot of work to do for this album. You've got your future to think of."

"My future?" she asked. "I sort of thought I was living my future. You know how much I love teaching music to the kids, Pop."

"I know that, lassie, but you've got an opportunity

to really accomplish something with your music. I don't think it would hurt anything to curb your usual routine for a few weeks. This could mean the big time for you."

"What if I don't want the big time, Pop?" She felt the usual tightness that constricted her chest when she considered moving out of this beloved apartment. She loved being home, loved being close to her family.

Her father scoffed at her comment. "Not want to share that talent of yours with the world? Why on earth would you throw away what you've been blessed with? I've never heard such foolishness. You have a true gift, Ruby. I must confess I've often felt guilty about my role in halting your mother's career."

Sunday had met Patrick Collins when she was singing in a small pub in Ireland. Pop swore to this day her mother would have been more famous than Madonna if he hadn't snatched her off the stage to make her a wife and mother. Teagan could remember her mother laughing whenever Pop told the tale, dismissing it as an outright lie, though Teagan knew Sunday had reveled in her husband's unwavering belief in her talent.

"Your pop and Riley have just been reworking the schedule in the restaurant so we can work on our songs," Sky said. "They've very graciously reassigned your shifts so we can have plenty of quiet time up here. Alone."

Teagan's heart skipped a beat as she pondered whether he'd really stressed the word *alone* or she'd just imagined he had. "Oh Pop, I couldn't do that to you and the others. I refuse to leave you short-handed."

"Short-handed?" Pop repeated, shaking his head emphatically. "It's the slow season, Ruby. You know that. Joyce has been complaining about her lack of work hours for weeks. She'll be delighted to have a chance to pick up some extra pay."

Joyce Bernard was one of the few people not related to the Collins family who worked in the restaurant. She'd been a waitress for them for nearly a decade and she would most certainly like the extended work hours, as her husband had recently been laid off. Keira and Ewan had been working like mad to give Joyce as many hours as they could afford to help keep her family afloat.

"Oh, that's true." Teagan struggled to think of some other argument against she and Sky being left alone, but nothing came to her. She'd lost the bet and now she had to pay the piper…with her father standing over her to make sure she did.

"In fact," Pop wiped his mouth and turned to Riley, "it's time you and I got downstairs to give Ewan and Tris a hand, missy. The lunch rush is probably gearing up by now."

"You're leaving? Now?" Teagan asked, cursing the alarm in her voice.

Pop looked at her strangely while Riley rolled her eyes with frustration. "Later, sis," she said dismissively, shooing her father along.

Clearly Riley was not going to be helpful in her attempts to fight temptation in regards to Sky Mitchell. She watched Sky as he rose from the counter with a wicked grin on his face. Yep, he had her number all right.

"Don't look so scared, gypsy. I'm not the Big Bad Wolf and I'll only bite when you beg me to."

He continued coming toward her and she fought against taking a step away. "Don't hold your breath, rock star. Pleading is something you'll never hear from these lips." She grinned, pleased with the strength of her denial. She could do this.

He reached out and pulled her toward him. She reached up, intent on grasping his ear, but he'd grown wise to that move and he captured her hands, pulling them behind her back. Her breasts were pressed flat to his chest and she wondered why the fear that had plagued her since dawn suddenly evaporated. Something about being held in Sky's arms felt right, comforting. God, she really was lost.

"Sky." She meant the word to be chastising, but it fell short of that mark when his intent became clear. He swallowed her next breath with his lips, claiming her mouth in a manner that was the complete opposite of last night's easy explorations. Today, he laid siege, plundering and demanding her surrender. He wasn't taking prisoners. He was playing to win.

She fought against his grip on her wrists until he relinquished her hands. Once free, she wrapped her arms around his neck, running her fingers through his thick, dark hair. Her touch spurred him on and she felt him pushing her backward, toward the couch. Neither of them came up for air as she lay on her back on the sofa, Sky's large frame covering hers in an instant.

Every part of their bodies touched as he continued his assault on her lips. His hands moved under her blouse and she gasped when he enveloped the sensitive globes with his palms, pushing against her tight nipples until she wanted to scream. The sensations he evoked with his lips and hands traveled down her body and her hips gyrated wildly against his denim-clad cock, her pussy demanding attention.

One of his hands left her breast and she whimpered until she felt the material of her skirt being lifted. Sky's hand brushed the side of her thigh and she felt the knowledge of what he intended to do crash down on her.

Holy hell. What was she doing?

"Stop." She turned her head to the side, fighting to say the word when his lips descended on her neck. "Sky. Please stop."

Her words, stronger this time, seemed to penetrate through the thick sexual air that surrounded and threatened to choke them. He leaned up on his elbows, the sensuous feeling of his weight on her body driving her mad.

No, she thought.

"No," she said.

"No?" he asked, clearly confused by the multitude of mixed signals she was sending. She'd let things go way too far.

"I'm so sorry," she said. "I just can't do this. Not with you. Not here. Not now."

He seemed to consider her words and she was relieved when a crooked, amused grin covered his face.

"Maybe I am the Big Bad Wolf. I sort of jumped on you, didn't I?"

"I wasn't exactly fighting you off. Guess I'd make a lousy Little Red Riding Hood."

"I don't know," Sky said as he pushed himself away from her. She missed the sensation of him lying on top of her the instant he reached down to pull her into a sitting position. "You sure do have the coloring for the part."

They sat together on the couch in silence for several moments and Teagan sensed he was trying as hard as she was to pull it together, to beat down the horny beasts clamoring for release.

"I don't jump into bed with strangers," she said when the silence became unbearable. Then she instantly regretted her words, realizing how they sounded. "I mean, I'm not implying that *you* do. I'm just saying that I don't."

"I understand, Teagan. In fact, I think with that line you sort of solidified my respect for you. It's been growing since last night and dammit, now you've got it —hook, line and sinker."

She laughed at his apparent disgruntlement. "Respect is a bad thing?"

"I really want to fuck you."

"Now you've lost me."

"I got out of a shitty relationship a while back. Since then, I've been keeping my affairs light, emotionless. Rather disrespectful of me, I guess you could say."

"Not if the women you were—" She struggled to find her next word. She was certain Sky was discussing sex, but she couldn't bring herself to imagine him with another woman in that way. "If the women you were dating knew it was all just for fun, then that's not really disrespectful."

"They knew where I stood," he said. "I just don't think that stopped them from wanting and hoping for more."

"Ah, I see." She'd been right to stop him. Her body was currently reading her the riot act, but her mind was sighing with relief. She'd obviously had a near miss because, after talking to Sky, she knew there was no way she could give her body to him and hope to retain her pride as well.

But, dammit, she was chomping at the bit to learn more. Riley was right. There was no doubt in her mind Sky could teach her all sorts of things she desperately wanted to learn. "I think I may be in over my head here."

"Join the club," he murmured.

The awkward silence descended again.

"So what do we do now?" she asked.

"Now, I guess we write music."

WHEN SKY GLANCED out the window, he was startled to realize night had fallen. He and Teagan had thrown themselves into their work and it dawned on him the pent-up passion of their unfinished interlude this afternoon seemed to have made its way out and onto the pages before them.

Teagan wasn't just a good songwriter. She was a brilliant one. He'd worked with countless musicians in the past, but none of them had her talent, her ability to create words and melodies that jumped off the page. He was also enthralled by her skill with the guitar. He'd spent the better part of the day watching her fingers strum the strings with a soft touch that left his cock stiff as a pike. A few minutes in the shower would have relieved at least a bit of his need, but he couldn't make himself leave her for even that long. He was afraid of breaking the spell surrounding them. He'd written more music in the past six hours than he had in the last six months. She'd broken through his writer's block and he felt rejuvenated, refreshed, ready to take on the world. They'd made decent headway on at least three songs and he was certain each and every one of them would be a hit.

She put the guitar down and reached up, kneading her neck in an attempt to rub out some of the stiffness. He rose and stepped behind her, massaging the kinks.

She leaned her head forward and groaned. "I can't tell you how good that feels."

He grinned, and then looked toward the stairs that led to the pub below. Her siblings had come up at various points during the day. Riley had brought them both a plate of tonight's dinner special. He looked at the empty plates on the coffee table and tried to remember consuming the food. At the time, they'd been so engrossed on finessing the words of the chorus they'd been working on, he honestly couldn't recall now what they'd eaten.

"What time is it?" she muttered as he continued to rub her delicate neck. She was soft, her skin so pale she was almost translucent. He glanced at the clock on the wall.

"Just after ten."

"Pop and Riley should be up in a bit," she said. "Tris and Ewan will keep the pub open until midnight. Guess we should clean up."

He looked around at the living room. "How the hell did it get so messy?"

She laughed. "You seem to share my bad habit of scattering paper everywhere when you write. My family goes mad when I'm in the zone because I tend to lay waste to every room in the apartment."

"In the zone? Is that where we were?"

"Wasn't it?"

"Yeah, I guess it was. I generally do my writing alone. I don't think I've ever been in the zone with another person." He had composed a few lighthearted numbers with the other members of The Universe, typically when they were drinking on the tour bus and feeling punchy late at night. They'd even released a couple of them and they were quite popular party songs. All the serious music the band performed, he'd written on his own.

"I've never been there with someone else either." She rose from her chair and turned to face him. "It was nice having the company in there." She rose up on tiptoe to place a soft kiss on his cheek. For reasons he couldn't explain, the platonic nature of her light buss pissed him off. When she began to retreat, he reached out and pulled her back to him, roughly.

"Sky."

"There are limits to everything, gypsy." They were nose to nose, but he refused to let her go.

"What's that supposed to mean?"

"You don't want to have sex. We won't. But that doesn't mean I won't kiss you. Real kisses. I have limits, too, and the main one is I can't sit beside you day in and day out and not touch you. It's just not possible." He bent down and punctuated his words with a hard, deep kiss.

"So we're going to draw a line in the sand and hope the tide doesn't wash it away? I don't think I can handle this, Sky. I'm not as experienced at casual affairs as you are."

"Even if I promise it'll be fun?"

She laughed at his joke, as he'd intended. He wasn't about to get into a discussion of casual anything with her. For one thing, he was really starting to like her, which was playing havoc with his plans to seduce her. He hadn't lied about respecting her. She was one of the most genuinely giving people he'd ever met. Her work at the preschool and the nursing home proved that and he'd spent most of the morning listening to her sister and pop sing her praises. The funny thing was, he didn't think they even knew they were doing it. They'd just drop these little tidbits about Teagan into normal conversation without realizing they were drawing a picture in his mind of an incredibly kind woman.

Teagan needs to find someone else to serve at the soup kitchen Saturday.

Did Teagan remember to take back the laundry she'd done for the widow across the street who'd had her water turned off?

Mrs. O'Malley called to see if Teagan would pick up a prescription for her on the way home from the preschool.

All day long he'd listened to their commonplace chatter and with each word, he found himself more and more fascinated. He nuzzled his nose into her neck, breathing in her scent—honeysuckle?

"You're incorrigible, Sky."

"Incorrigible in a 'you can't keep you hands off me' kind of way?"

"Argh," she groaned. "Why do I have the sneaking suspicion if I looked up 'player' in the dictionary, I'd find a picture of you?"

"If that's true, then it merely proves my point. This will be fun. Play with me, Teagan." His words came out more seriously than he'd intended. He'd meant to keep things light and fun and he fully intended to ignore the part of him that said he wanted to be closer to her for reasons far more important than just sex.

"I want a promise from you, Sky," she said, resisting him when he tried to pull her in for another kiss.

"What promise?"

"Promise you won't let things go too far. I mean, I know how to say no—"

"So I've learned," he interjected.

She grinned. "Promise you'll always stop when I say we've gone far enough."

He loosened his grip on her waist, reaching instead

for her hands. "Teagan, I would never take advantage of you. Never take you without your consent. I promise."

"Okay. Teach me something fun."

Her words—followed up by her lips rubbing against his cheek—opened the floodgates and the desires he'd been holding at bay all day emerged with a vengeance.

"What about your pop and sister?" he asked.

She glanced back at the clock. "It's ten fifteen. The restaurant closes in fifteen minutes and then they'll clean up. We have about an hour."

He grinned, thinking of all the things he could do to her in an hour. "Just the same, I'd prefer to give us a bit of leeway should they finish early." He took her hand and led her to her bedroom. It was tidy and tastefully decorated considering how different she and Riley were. He'd almost expected to find a line drawn down the middle, one side covered in peace signs and flowers, the other decorated with pictures of naked men on Harleys.

"Which bed is yours?" he asked.

When she hesitated, he touched her face, drawing her gaze to him. "I meant what I said. I stand by my promises."

She pointed to the twin bed on the right and he shook his head. It was going to be a tight fit. He let her lead him to the bed, nearly choking when she sat down in front of him. Her face was level with his cock and he watched with disbelief as she reached up to stroke him through the tight jeans.

"Looks crowded in there," she said, grinning up at him.

"Yeah, well, it's gonna have to stay crowded. You let him out and all bets are off. Tonight is about teaching you how to play. How to have fun."

She looked as if she wanted to argue so he cut her off at the pass, kneeling before her and pulling her into a long, wet kiss. He loved the taste and texture of her mouth. Her soft lips and sweet smells reminded him of Sunday dinners at home after months spent on the road. Her hands caressed his face and he savored the rough feel of the calluses left on her fingertips from years of playing the guitar.

He decided to do a bit of exploring and slowly slid his hands beneath her loose shirt, his palms itching to hold her breasts again. They filled his hands nicely, the perfect size, and he swallowed her cries when he lightly cupped and squeezed the fleshy mounds. He continued the kiss, playing with her breasts until the temptation, the need to see them, grew too great.

"I'm going to take off your shirt," he whispered when he pulled his lips away to taste her cheeks, her neck. Grasping the hem, he pulled the filmy material over her head and was greeted by the vision of some of the sexiest underwear he'd ever seen.

"Jesus," he murmured, a smile escaping as he studied her deep violet and pink bra. Her breasts were pushed up and peeking over the top. She was a veritable rainbow even under her clothing. A flush covered her chest and he glanced up at her face, watching as the blush colored her cheeks as well.

She put her hands on her face to hide it. "Curse of a true redhead. Damn blushing."

"I like it," he admitted. It had been a long time since he'd made a woman blush. The innocence of the gesture was captivating.

"The bra or the blush?" she asked, her voice laced with humor.

"Both, Ruby."

She giggled at his irreverent use of her father's pet name. "Leave it to you to take something sweet and innocent and twist it into something completely sexual."

He slipped the straps of her bra off her shoulders, tugging the lacy material down until her rosy nipples slipped out. "Jackpot," he whispered. She started to laugh, but the sound was cut off on a harsh gasp when he took one of the tight nubbins into his mouth and sucked.

"Oh God," she said. Her hands clasped his head, her fingers threading through his hair almost painfully. It was clear she didn't know what she was doing, but he felt even more blood rush to his rock-hard cock. Damn, but he loved it rough. He sucked on her nipple harder and was rewarded with a sexy groan. He reached up and pinched her other nipple, wondering if she would be averse to a bit of the rough stuff herself. She threw her head back as he squeezed and he wondered for a moment if she wasn't actually on the verge of an orgasm.

"Teagan?" he asked.

"That feels so good," she said before he could question her response. "No one's ever—"

Her words faded away on a loud gasp when he repeated the motion. He switched sides, sucking on the opposite breast. When he nipped at the tight tip, she nearly bucked off the bed. The woman was a firecracker, poised and ready to blow.

He moved quickly, dragging his hands under her skirt while sucking on her breast. He wondered if she realized what he was doing until she spread her legs apart, offering herself to his wandering fingers.

He could feel the dampness of her pussy through her panties, but he didn't trust himself to remove them from her completely so he merely thrust the material between her legs aside, dragging two fingers along her drenched slit.

She trembled and moaned, but he was determined to hold to his promise. "Teagan."

Her head rested on his shoulder, her body shaking with need. He wanted to give her what she wanted, but he had to be sure. "Teagan, look at me."

She lifted her head, the green in her eyes reminding him of a forest at dawn. "I want to make you come with my fingers. Just my fingers, I promise."

"Hurry," she whispered and he grinned. He kissed her lightly as he slowly pushed one finger into her pussy. She cried out and he marveled at how tightly she clamped his finger. For a moment, he cursed the promise he'd made. This woman would feel like heaven around his cock.

He pushed his hips against her bed, trying to find

some pressure for himself, something to relieve the ache building in his balls. He pulled his finger out and added a second, using the two digits to slowly fuck Teagan into oblivion. It only took a few shallow thrusts and the pressure of his thumb on her clit to push her over. Her climax seemed to radiate from every part of her body as she trembled in his arms. Her inner muscles throbbed almost painfully against his fingers and he pressed his cock into her bed frame harder, her orgasm threatening to push him into one of his own.

He was shocked when he felt her hand drift down to touch the front of his jeans, applying more of the pressure he needed so desperately. He looked at her, confused until she spoke.

"Close your eyes. I'll help you," she whispered, rubbing her hand along the front placket of his pants. His eyes drifted shut of their own accord under her talented fingers.

"Imagine I'm on my knees in front of you. I've got your jeans open and I'm taking your cock out." She squeezed him through his jeans just below the head and he moaned. The hot breath accompanying her words nearly scorched his cheek as she whispered in his ear all the things he wanted her to do to him.

"I'm taking you in my mouth now. You're pushing your cock between my lips." She pushed again, harder this time. "You're fucking my mouth, moving in and out, so hard, so fast. I'm swallowing the head of your cock now. So deep. You're so deep." Her words, the images she drew, were driving him mad. He began to push against her hand, lacing his fingers with hers, holding her in place as he thrust faster and faster.

"God," he groaned. "I'm going to come."

"Give it to me," she whispered. "Feed me. I want to swallow your cum. All of it."

"Christ," he cried, his cock erupting, the sticky semen coating his boxers. "Fuck." He struggled to catch his breath as her arms held him, his head resting between her gorgeous tits.

When he'd gathered his wits about him, he looked up to find her studying him anxiously. "I...I didn't think it was fair that you should suffer tonight because of me and my old-fashioned principles."

Her words triggered something in his mind and a thought—a terrible, obvious thought—clicked into place. "Teagan. Are you a virgin?"

She blushed again, this time her discomfort obvious as she bit her lower lip.

"You are." The answer was written on her face. Christ, she was innocent?

"Don't look at me like that." She pushed him away and stalked across the room. Even with her back to him, he could see she was trying to return her bra to rights before she put her blouse back on.

He stood slowly, his pants uncomfortable with the sticky semen coating them. "Like what?"

"Like you've just committed some ghastly crime. I may not have done the actual deed, but believe me, I've done plenty of other stuff. How the hell do you think I know about blowjobs?"

He pictured her sucking another man's cock and his

vision suddenly clouded red. "Is that right? So what we just did—"

"Wasn't anything new to me," she finished.

His eyes narrowed. It may not have been new to her, but it sure as hell felt new to him. "I see."

"Just because I'm saving myself for the right man doesn't mean I'm not having a bit of fun along the way."

He took a step closer. "So my lips on your breasts, my fingers in your pussy, that was all just a run-of-the-mill evening for you?"

She sucked in a breath and he saw it the moment she realized the error of her words. "I didn't mean it that way."

"You have a habit of saying things you don't mean, gypsy. Since all those things we just did were so commonplace, it's clear I'm going to have to put my energies into finding some different, unique experiences for you. I'd hate for you to feel as if you hadn't gotten your money's worth."

"You're angry and I can understand that, Sky, but—"

"Tomorrow night. Ten o'clock."

"What?"

"Tomorrow night. Same time, right here. I'm going to introduce you to things you didn't even know existed. Good night, gypsy."

"Sky—" she started, but he refused to give up the last word.

"Tomorrow," he repeated as he closed the door to her bedroom behind him.

<h1 style="text-align:center">Chapter Five</h1>

The following day crept by at a snail's pace as Teagan waited for ten o'clock to arrive. Her trepidation affected her work with Sky on the music, but when she'd pointed that fact out, he'd remained unmoved and unconcerned. He insisted he would be in her room at ten tonight and he didn't give a shit if they wrote a single note.

Of course, their work on the music would have been ruined anyway by the constant ringing of Sky's cell phone. Apparently his number had been leaked to the press and after the twentieth call, he'd turned the damn thing off, furious at the invasion of his privacy. She had felt a twinge of sympathy for him, as he certainly did seem to live his life under a microscope.

At nine she'd called it quits, claiming fatigue, and Sky had simply laughed when she said she was going to bed…alone. As she'd slunk down the hall to her room, he'd called out that he would see her later.

Now she lay in her bed, staring at the bright red numbers on the digital clock, fighting to fall asleep. Why couldn't she be like Riley? She'd tossed and turned for an hour, trying to deny the fact that her body was clamoring for Sky's arrival. She'd poked the tiger last night and she would be lucky if she wasn't mauled in the aftermath.

The clock flashed ten and, as if by magic, the door to her bedroom opened. She closed her eyes, pretending to be asleep and ignoring the fact he'd turned the lights on. Sky chuckled softly as he sat on the edge of her bed.

"You aren't fooling anybody with that lame deep-breathing routine."

She sighed and sat up. "You know, I apologized for what I said last night, Sky." She'd said she was sorry about a thousand times today.

"And I appreciate that. Now take off your pajamas."

"No," she said.

His eyes narrowed. "Don't say that unless you really mean it, Teagan."

She remembered the promise she'd solicited from him and she fell silent.

"Oh no, gypsy. That's not fair. Tell me you want this."

Did she want this? Shit. She'd spent the majority of her day stressing out over what he would do. So much so that she'd lost track of the rest of her emotions. She had no idea what he would do to her, but now that she considered the fact, she supposed it didn't matter. She wanted him to touch her, to teach her, to—please God —give her another one of those freaking orgasms. The rest of her anxieties faded away in the face of that.

"I don't want you to leave."

He grinned. It was the easy-going, fun smile she'd come to adore in just the short time they'd known each other and her fears melted away in an instant.

He bent down and kissed her gently. "You're beautiful," he murmured and she smiled.

"And you're a player," she teased.

"A rock star," he added with a chuckle.

"So rock my world, rock star," she dared. His eyes darkened at her taunt, the look hot enough to singe her hair.

"I want to see you naked. Completely naked."

She sucked in a nervous breath. She'd certainly been seen in various states of undress with past boyfriends, but she'd never been totally nude in a well-lit room in front of a man. "You know," she said, "the freckles don't stop at my face."

"I noticed that last night. I think your freckles are hot. Now stop stalling."

She sat up in bed and pushed the covers off. She started with the part he'd already seen, shrugging her T-shirt over her head. He gripped her waist once she'd tossed the shirt aside and studied her so closely she felt the cursed blushing start.

"Your turn," she said, gesturing to his shirt. He pulled his shirt off without hesitation and she followed his lead, perusing him at her leisure. She'd seen him without his shirt on the first night they'd met. Unfortunately, she'd been too fixated on the absurdity of him flitting around in her skirt to fully appreciate the view. Now, she was seeing him as clear as day and the sight took her breath away. Smooth, tanned skin, chiseled-in-stone pecs and tight brown nipples she couldn't resist leaning forward to lick.

He groaned as her tongue teased the small disks, his hands engulfing her head, holding her in place. "Jesus, that feels good."

Over and over she kissed, nipped and licked the sensitive flesh until he pulled her head away, leaning over to capture her mouth in a hungry kiss. He pressed her backward onto the mattress and covered her once more. There was something very addictive to being sheltered beneath the strength of his hard body. She ran her hands over his chest, his arms, his back. She couldn't touch enough of him as the heat in the small room continued to rise. He pushed his covered cock into the vee of her thighs and she whimpered with relief at the glorious force.

She heard rather than saw him take off his belt, shocked when he engulfed her hands in his above her head. He laid the strip of leather beside her on the bed.

"I'm going to bind your hands."

His words were spoken simply, matter-of-factly, yet the impact hit her like the shot from a gun marking the beginning of a fifty-yard dash and her heart raced so fast she feared it would burst.

"Sky," she started.

"The promise still stands, Teagan. You say no and it all stops."

She nodded. She trusted him. "Okay."

"Here," he said, rising and pulling her up as well, "let's get these pants off."

Her hands stopped him when he reached for the waistband and he looked at her questioningly. "What is it?"

"The red hair is sort of like the freckles. Everywhere."

He laughed. "Another benefit to hooking up with a wild Irish gypsy." He lightly pushed her hands away, pulling her pants down until they hit her ankles. She kicked them off. "No panties?"

She crinkled her nose. "Can't stand sleeping in them."

"Me either," he said and she tried to imagine sleeping with Sky, both of them naked and wrapped in each other's arms. "Don't do that," he said.

"Do what?"

"Undress me with your eyes."

She laughed as he threw her words from their first conversation in the pub back at her. "Can I do it with my hands?"

"Not if you plan to end this night still a virgin." He turned her around, facing the bed, and she yelped when he placed a firm slap on her bare ass.

"What was that for?" she asked, rubbing the sore spot with her hand.

"Being cheeky. Lie down on your stomach and put your hands above your head."

She wanted to refute his "cheeky" comment, but his commands erased every thought from her head except the belt and the binding. She lay down, the position driving home to her just how hard her heart was pounding. She could swear the mattress was shaking under the force of it.

"What are you going to do?" she asked.

"Do you really want to know or do you prefer the element of surprise?"

She considered his question. She hated surprises. All the hours she'd spent stressing out this morning only reinforced that point. She'd worried and fretted until she couldn't function.

"I want to know," she said. He sat down beside her, his weight on the small bed pushing the mattress down and causing her bare hip to brush against the rough denim of his jeans.

He bent forward until his chest pressed against her back and she shivered as he whispered in her ear. "I'm going to tie you up, spank you, and then fuck your pussy and ass with my fingers. Any questions?"

"Holy shit," she murmured. "I changed my mind. I want to be surprised."

He laughed. "Too late. I'm not changing the melody this late in the song. You're just going to have to be a good little virgin and take it."

"If you call me a virgin again, I'm twisting your ear."

He shuddered with mock fear and she grinned. "So noted," he said.

He picked up his belt and looped the soft leather around her wrists. "I'm not going to pull this too tight," he said, as he knotted the free end to her bed frame.

"Mainly because I don't want to hurt you. I just want you to have a sense of being helpless, at my mercy." He dropped his voice to a teasing, raspy whisper following the pronouncement by singing a few notes of a horror song. "Da, da, daaaa."

She giggled, trying to escape his bonds. While the leather wasn't tight enough to cut into her wrists, she was definitely bound. She wouldn't be able to get free until he released her. "You seem to like this part too much." Her words were light, but his response wasn't.

"More than I care to admit. There's something wild about you that makes me want to tie you to my side and never let you go."

He pulled back at the end of his confession and she sensed he'd said more than he wanted to. More than he was comfortable sharing. Her chest constricted with the thought, the hope that her cocky rock star really wasn't playing a game with her. Then she remembered his comments about his casual affairs. They would write their songs, explore each other's bodies and then, as sure as the sun would rise tomorrow, he'd leave. She forced herself to remember that. She burned that knowledge on her heart, praying the words engraved there would protect her from forgetting that simple truth.

"Touch me," she urged, anxious to erase the painful thoughts with sensation.

Her head lay against her pillow, facing him, and she could see him shrugging off his own uneasy feelings. He raised his hand, resting it on her bare bum, and she narrowed her eyes, recalling his words. "I haven't been a bad girl," she said. "You have no reason to spank me."

He nodded slowly and she thought for a moment he was adjusting his game plan. At least, until he spoke. "You know, some people consider spanking a form of foreplay. The edge of pain turns them on, arouses them."

She couldn't imagine that being true. "I have a low threshold for pain."

"Is that right?" he asked. "Should we test that theory? If you hate it, you only have to say stop."

His face betrayed his hope that she wouldn't refuse this request. She remembered his rough touches last night as he'd sucked and bit her breasts. At the time, she'd been too out of her mind with need to register the fact that his mouth was hurting her. In a very sexy way.

She wiggled her ass. "Spank me," she whispered, surprised to realize the husky, needy voice speaking was hers.

He didn't smile as she expected but she could see how much her request pleased him. His hand drifted down to his jeans, tugging against the constricting material. His hard-on looked bigger than it had the previous night and she thought he must be in pain.

"Unzip your pants," she said. "Let me see you."

He shook his head. "I can't." The words were spoken in a short, clipped breath and she realized exactly how much restraint he was exercising to give her what she wanted without breaking his promise. She felt a tiny piece of her heart break away and she knew it now belonged to him. Her mind screamed *danger*, but she couldn't call a halt now. She simply couldn't step off this path until she saw what lay at the end.

She was too lost in her thoughts to realize he'd raised his hand, too preoccupied with her worries to see what was coming.

"Ouch!" she yelled when his hand came down hard on her left buttocks. Her reaction fell on deaf ears as he lifted his hand, spanking her three more times. He certainly wasn't pulling his punches; his slaps were firm and painful. Her ass felt as if he'd set it on fire and for a moment, she considered stopping him. Then, just as a brush fire jumps, the flames he'd lit on her ass turned inward and her pussy began to spark, then burn.

"God," she gasped.

"Yes or no," he said between blows, his hand resting lightly on her sore ass.

"Yes," she cried. "God, yes."

He continued the spanking for several moments, breaking up the blows with soft, gentle rubs that only stoked the fire higher. She felt herself anticipating his swings, raising her ass to meet his hand as it lowered.

She trembled after one particularly hard smack, rubbing her legs together, trying to create the friction her body was demanding.

"Open your legs," he commanded and she complied, screaming with relief as he drove two hard fingers deep inside her. "So wet," he murmured, his fingers moving fast within her.

Her climax rumbled through her like a freight train

and she shuddered for several moments afterward, feeling very much as if she'd been run over by a bus.

She suspected she'd drifted off for a few minutes. Sky was lying beside her and it wasn't until she reached over to touch his handsome face that she realized he'd released her. His hand lay limp on her ass and she grinned as she recalled how much she'd enjoyed his spanking. She never would have suspected such a seemingly violent act could feel so…well, wonderful.

"You back with me?" he asked, confirming that she had indeed been unconscious.

"Mmm hmm." She closed her eyes, overcome with a contentment she'd never experienced. She smiled to herself as the thought grew. She'd never experienced anything like this.

"That's a pretty smile," he whispered. "Wonder if I can build on it." His hand rubbed her sore ass for a few moments before he sat up, kneeling by her hips. "Get up on your hands and knees. I promised you one more experience."

Her foggy mind tried to recall what he'd said and for an instant she thought he was mistaken. Then his words came back to her as she rose up and for a moment she considered crying halt.

I'm going to fuck your pussy and ass with my fingers.

Any thoughts of escape were washed away as he slid his fingers through her still-damp slit. She didn't think she'd ever been so wet, so aroused in her life. "Sky," she said. Her voice dropped off when he slid two fingers into her pussy. She was instantly thrust back into his well of seduction, immersed in the incredible feelings this man could provoke with just his hand. She thrust toward his fingers, trying to set the pace, take him deeper, but as soon as she moved, he pulled out.

"Don't stop," she whimpered.

He moved on the bed until he knelt between her legs. "Bend your arms. Lower your chest to the bed but keep your ass up. I'm not finished playing."

She did as he asked, certain she should be mortified at the image she must be presenting. She could feel his gaze on her bare flesh and the mere thought caused her to tremble. God, the man was playing her body better than he played his guitar.

His fingers drifted from her pussy to her anus and again she fought against denying him. This was unknown, forbidden territory. If only her damn curiosity weren't so powerful. It was overriding every other part of her mind that was saying they'd gone far enough.

The tip of his index finger, wet from her juices, slowly pushed into the tight ring of muscle. She couldn't hold back the small cry that escaped her lips.

"Does that hurt?" he asked.

"Not yet."

He chuckled. "That spanking I just gave you had to hurt. I didn't hear you complain about that. Maybe you'll like this pain too."

She doubted that very much, but she didn't refute his words. He dragged his fingers back to her pussy, gathering up more of her juices. He was trying to make this good for her. She could appreciate that fact even if she wasn't sure she wanted it. This time, he pushed his finger in farther. She squirmed as she felt the second knuckle pass. Once his entire finger was buried in her ass, he paused and she remembered to breathe.

He wiggled the finger inside her and she gasped at the unexpected wealth of new sensations. This touch felt very different from that of his fingers in her pussy, but it was no less exciting, no less searing.

His finger began to retreat and she felt her muscles contracting, trying to hold him inside. "Jesus," he muttered. "You like this."

It wasn't a question. It was a simple statement of fact. When only the tip of his finger remained, he began the return trip. His movements were slow, measured and easy, but soon that wasn't enough. He'd definitely awakened some latent needs inside her. Needs that demanded force, power and yes, dear God, an edge of pain. She wasn't sure what she was becoming but at this moment, need outweighed everything else in her life.

"Fuck my ass," she demanded. "Harder. Faster."

His finger stopped as she spoke the words and then he granted her wish. His finger plowed inside her and she felt pinches of discomfort laced with incredible vibrations that claimed her from the waist down. With his free hand, he peppered her ass with short, hard smacks and she cried out, biting down on her pillow to drown out the screams.

Harder and harder he drove his finger inside her ass.

"More," she gasped.

He used his other hand on her clit, pushing and

pinching the distended flesh until she quivered violently on the bed, crying out her climax. The strength of the orgasm claimed her exhausted body and she felt herself drifting into the blessed darkness as his finger slid out of her.

SKY TURNED onto his back on the couch, fluffing the pillow under his head once more, praying to find a comfortable position. He'd come out to the living room to sleep when he worried his tossing and turning would disturb Ewan. His mind whirled over the night's events as he tried to figure out what in the hell he was supposed to do now.

Teagan wasn't fitting into his preconceived ideas of what his future looked like. In fact, the woman was turning his world on its ear. Two days ago, he'd been toying with the idea of leaving The Universe. Within minutes of meeting her, he'd decided to definitely leave the band and had shanghaied her into helping him write the songs for his solo album. That was all he'd wanted from her. Well, that and maybe a roll in the hay.

Now he was suffering from the worst case of blue balls in the history of man because of that damn promise she'd extracted from him. A promise he sure as hell wouldn't break now that he knew she was a virgin, hell-bent on holding out for true love. Every man on the planet knew not to fuck with a twenty-six-year-old virgin unless marriage was the goal. And that was something definitely *not* in his plans for a happy future.

Christ. All he'd wanted was a solo career and a solo life. Holly had taught him all too well that love wasn't meant to last for people who'd opted for fame and fortune. No relationship could handle the strain of the paparazzi or a life on the road for long. Hell, Teagan would hate the constant flashing of cameras in her face. He couldn't do that to her even if things between them progressed to that point. Which they wouldn't.

The thought of Holly sent his mind in a different direction as he wondered if she was the person siccing the paparazzi on him at every turn. He'd always been plagued by the cameras, but never to this extreme. Lately he felt as if he had a giant target on his back. Before yesterday's successful writing with Teagan, they'd annoyed him so much he'd been unable to write much of anything of value. Teagan had changed that. He smiled as he pictured her playing the guitar in those long, colorful skirts and he wondered when he'd begun to see hippie garb as sexy. She was definitely something special, something unique.

He shook his head. He was here to write music for the album and perform the last concert with The Universe. Once that was done, it was adios Baltimore and goodbye Teagan. He rubbed his chest, wondering why the thought of leaving her behind caused an actual physical ache inside him.

Two days. He'd known her two days. He was just overwrought, overtired and she'd come at a time when he was feeling vulnerable, out of control. Holly had fucked with his head, the paparazzi was driving him fucking nuts and he'd just fought World War III with Marty on the phone this morning after he'd broken the news of his decision to strike out on his own. He'd finish the songs and get the hell out of here. No doubt after a few days away from Teagan, he'd be his old cocky, womanizing self again. With that consoling thought, he closed his eyes and forced sleep to come.

He'd just drifted off when he felt a tug at the waistband of his sweatpants. He opened his eyes, shocked to discover Teagan leaning over the couch.

"What are you doing?" he whispered.

"I'm dressed," she said as if that was the answer to his question.

"So?"

"So get up. There's no way I'm not playing fair anymore, Sky. You've given me two nights of incredible orgasms and you've taken nothing for yourself. I'll leave my clothes on, but I'm telling you right now, I'm sucking your cock and that's all there is to it."

He'd heard some propositions in his life, but like everything else about the woman, her comment left him teetering on the line between laughter and begging. He'd sell his soul to the devil to feel her lips on his aching cock.

"Since you've worded it that way, refusal seems to be pointless, doesn't it?"

"Come on."

"Where are we going?"

"The office," she whispered.

There was a tiny room off the living room that the

family used as an office. It was only large enough for a desk and bookshelf, but the door locked. He grinned at her ingenuity. Clearly, she'd learned to improvise when she needed privacy, given the fact she lived in an overcrowded apartment with her siblings.

She closed and locked the door, leading him to the office chair. He could see she was pleased with his acquiescence as she struggled to relieve him of his pants.

"Here," he said. "Let me help." The idea of Teagan on her knees before him left Sky slightly lightheaded in his exhaustion and he was surprised to notice his hands were shaking a bit. He pushed the sweatpants to his ankles and then sat back down with his knees spread apart. She knelt, moving closer and settling between his legs. Her hands teased the hair on his upper thighs as she looked at him.

"I lied," she said at last.

"About what?"

"About giving a blowjob. I've never done this. I only knew about it from a dirty book I read once."

He marveled for a moment over her honesty and then tried to figure out how the hell she was still single. Were the men on the East Coast blind and insane? "Are you sure you want to do this?" he asked.

"Oh hell yeah," she said so assuredly, he did laugh.

"Do you want directions?"

She shook her head. "Nope, I think I can figure it out. You'll tell me if I do something you don't like?"

"I don't think there's anything you could do that wouldn't knock my cock off, gypsy."

She grinned at his compliment and bent forward. She teased the tip of his cock with her tongue for several moments and he leaned his head back against the chair and started counting to a thousand by tens. She hadn't even taken him into her mouth and he was already afraid of coming too soon. The last two celibate nights spent watching her orgasm hadn't helped his stamina. Hell, a strong draft was likely to make him blow.

Her hands left his thighs, gripping the base of his hard flesh with firm, sure fingers. Fuck. So much for a novice. He'd have to get the title of that dirty book she'd read so he could write and thank the author. She took the head into her mouth, her hot breath tickling and tantalizing the sensitive nerve endings there. A groan escaped his lips and he noticed the sound spurred her on. She took him deeper as her grip on the base of his cock tightened. She was fucking doing everything right.

Her lips moved up and down his shaft as she started sucking him, fucking him with her gorgeous mouth.

"Faster," he said between gritted teeth. She increased her pace and her grip, torturing his cock with hard, firm motions that sent a rush of cum to his balls.

Christ. It was too fast but he couldn't hold off. Not when the image of her lovely red head bobbing up and down—

Fuck. He closed his eyes. He couldn't watch her and hope to hold on. He was surprised when her strong grip on his cock disappeared. His eyes flew open and he watched, spellbound, as she took even more of him into her mouth. The head of his cock hit the back of her throat and he groaned again. She was swallowing him. He was lost. His climax erupted like a volcano the moment she began to hum.

Holy mother of God. He only just managed to recall the fact they were surrounded by her family. Locked door or not, her brothers would definitely kick his ass for this. He swallowed back his loud cry as she drank down every drop of semen.

She held his cock in her mouth as it deflated and he was touched by the soothing way she caressed him as he fought to regain his wits.

"Come here," he said when he had the strength to move. He pulled her onto his lap, kissing her, tasting his essence on her lips and wondering what the fuck he was supposed to do now. Leaving her suddenly didn't seem like such an easy option.

Chapter Six

The rest of the week moved in a languid, easy pace. The Collins family was easy to be around. They all possessed a great sense of humor and he enjoyed the time spent in their midst very much. Tris and Ewan still eyed him with suspicion, although he'd made certain to hide his sexual attraction to their older sister when they were around. He and Teagan were both careful around her family, portraying themselves as nothing more than writing partners and friends.

During the afternoons and evenings when they were alone, they worked diligently on their songs, taking turns at the guitar. The music was evolving into something he suspected was surprising to them both. He'd never written better songs and he knew it. She mentioned the same held true for her. They were the perfect complement to each other professionally and, as each night revealed, physically.

Ten o'clock marked the end of their workday and

they spent the last hour before bed exploring each other's bodies, touching and kissing, giving and taking. He'd kept his promise and protected her virginity, although each night the temptation to lose himself in her body grew until he feared he'd lose his mind from wanting.

Teagan maintained part of her usual routine, singing at the pub over the weekend and Tuesday night. He'd sat at the bottom of the stairs, out of sight of the patrons, and listened to her as she performed. She'd gone to the nursing home twice, and this morning she'd left to teach her class at the preschool.

He dialed the phone to check in with Rod. He'd called him a couple nights ago to break the news to his friend about his decision to definitely leave The Universe.

"Hey, bud," Sky said when Rod answered the phone.

"Sky, what's up?"

"Nothing. I just called to see if you'd had a chance to stop by and check on my place." Rod often kept an eye on his house in Palm Springs when he was out of town.

"Yep. Slid by there yesterday and everything is just as it's supposed to be. Shame to see such a damn big house sitting empty for nine, ten months of the year."

Sky laughed. Rod had been trying to get him to sell the place for ages. Sky agreed that it was probably silly to keep a mansion that sat empty most of the time, but he liked the idea of having a place to call home.

"I'm not selling," he said and he heard Rod sigh.

"Do you know what the commission on that place would be?"

Sky thought for a moment he heard a bit of anger in his friend's voice and he wondered about his comment. "You need money? I know property sales have sucked lately. I could float you a loan."

Rod brushed his offer aside. "I'm fine, Sky. No worries. I'm just kidding. So, you still at the Irish pub?"

Sky had filled his friend in on his adventures with the paparazzi the previous week during their last call. "I'm still here."

"How are the songs coming?" his friend asked.

"Great. Freaking brilliant." Sky grinned as he heard Teagan's footsteps on the stairs, feeling like a teenager with a crush at the excitement he felt over seeing her again. "Hey listen, man. I've gotta get going. Thanks for looking after the place. I'll talk to you in a few days."

He hung up and watched as Teagan entered the room. His smile dimmed when he saw her pale, worried face.

"Teagan?" he asked. "What's wrong?"

"Outside. Cameras."

He moved quickly to the window, standing off to the side to peek down without being seen.

"They know you're here."

He was amazed by the sheer number of cameramen lining the sidewalk. He crossed the room and peered into the back alley. It was also jam-packed with press.

"How?"

She shrugged and he felt the same anger rise, the same frustration that besieged him whenever confronted with the paparazzi. "You must have some idea, Teagan. Who did you tell?"

Her eyes narrowed. "I didn't tell anyone."

"Well, I haven't talked to anyone. Someone in your family must have let it slip. Maybe Riley."

"She wouldn't do that. None of them would do that. They know how much your privacy means to you."

"Sure they wouldn't. You'd be amazed what an easy buck will make people do."

Teagan's face flushed and he cursed his harsh words, but he couldn't shake the idea that someone in the Collins family had betrayed him. He was surprised by how much that thought hurt.

"My family isn't like that," she insisted. "How do you know it wasn't your manager? He was pretty pissed off when you said you were leaving the band."

"He doesn't know I'm here."

"He's the one who sent you to Baltimore."

"A hotel in Baltimore, yes. He has no idea I've been staying here the last week."

"Your friend Rod knows about this place. He was here with you," she said.

"Rod wouldn't betray me."

"Oh right. You can say that about Rod and I'm supposed to accept it at face value, but when I tell you my family didn't tell anyone—"

"Dammit, Teagan. No one else knew I was here.

Fine. Let's say for argument's sake it wasn't your family. Who else could it have been? Mrs. Tibbs?"

"She didn't recognize you. I'm sure of that."

"Fine. One of your pop's old cronies. One of the men watching the contest."

She shook her head. "They don't know you're still here. As far as they're concerned, you went back to your hotel the night of the contest."

"Great. Well, that really narrows it down, doesn't it?"

"Holy fuck city," Riley said, stomping into the room with a police officer behind her. "Hell has officially broken loose outside."

Sky lifted his hand, gesturing to the stranger in their midst. "Well, look," he said, unable to hide the sarcasm in his tone. "Riley's brought home someone else who isn't supposed to know I'm here."

Teagan walked over to him angrily and for a moment he was torn between guarding his ears or his balls. She was truly pissed off. "Aaron is a friend, you asshole."

Aaron stepped over to him with his hand outstretched. "I'm Aaron Young. I'm a friend of the Collins family. It's a pleasure to meet you, Mr. Mitchell. I'm a big fan of The Universe."

Sky shook his hand, though his anger hadn't abated. "I assume Riley called you in to disperse the crowd out there. I should tell you——"

"Actually, she called me to help get you out of here. Those cameramen won't move until you do."

"I'm not sure how they know I'm here. I've been quite diligent about remaining out of sight."

Riley stepped forward, pointing out one of the living room windows. "One of the assholes down there managed to sweet-talk his way into an apartment across the street. He has a pretty good shot taken with a long-range lens of you and Teagan working on the couch in here. The jig is definitely up."

Pop came up the stairs and Sky could see weariness in the old man's face. "Shooed everyone out and locked the restaurant," he said. "Impossible to serve folks food and drinks with the crowd growing outside. Noise was unbearable and everyone was scrambling to get in. We were in danger of breaking the fire code for the number of people allowed in the place."

"I'm sorry, Pat," Sky said. "I didn't mean to disrupt your business." He knew in his heart of hearts the old man hadn't given away his location to the press. Teagan's pop was one in a million. He'd listened to their work in progress each afternoon, offering genuine advice and kind encouragement. He tended to look at Sky as if he'd offered his daughter the moon on a platter and he knew exactly how much her father wanted to see Teagan succeed in the music business. He wouldn't jeopardize her future for any amount of money.

"Oh, don't be silly, son. It's just a minor setback. I could use a day off and besides, do you know what this could mean for business when folks learn Sky Mitchell wrote all the songs on his next album in this pub? You can't buy advertising like that."

Sky grinned and hoped that proved to be true.

Tris and Ewan came upstairs, followed closely by Teagan's older sister, Keira.

"Sean and Will are downstairs guarding the doors," Keira announced. She looked at Aaron and smiled. "Thanks to your friends on the force, the press and the crowd have been pushed back across the street. I was afraid someone was going to get shoved through the window for a few minutes. We've got to figure a way to get Sky out of here and somewhere safe."

"I can see why you're so anxious to stay out of the public eye," Ewan said, sympathy written on his face. "This shit must drive you mad."

"I'm sorry about all the fuss," he repeated as all the siblings sat down in various chairs around the living room. He could see by the stress on their faces they were genuinely worried about him. He felt guilty about his earlier accusations. "I'll grab my stuff and call for a car. The hotel is better equipped to fend off the press."

"Now son, I appreciate you trying to remove yourself from the pub, but we need to look at the long-range plan. Have you and Teagan finished writing your songs?"

"No," he answered. "We've made some good headway on a few—"

"Well, then we need to find somewhere for the two of you to finish the job."

"She's not going to the hotel with him," Ewan interjected quickly.

Teagan rolled her eyes at her brother's overprotective comment. "I'm twenty-six, Ewan. I think I can decide where I go and don't go."

Tris scoffed. "You go to the hotel, I go to the hotel."

Pop shook his head. "I have to agree with your sister on this one, Tristan. She's an adult and, what's more, it's time she moved forward with her life."

Teagan's head popped up at her father's words and Sky could read the slightest bit of fear in her eyes at his pronouncement. He considered what that look could mean.

The family erupted into conversation, every Collins sibling throwing in their two cents on how they could get Teagan and Sky out of the apartment and away from the paparazzi.

"I have a suggestion," Aaron yelled, trying to be heard over the dull roar. The police officer had been quietly standing behind Riley since the conversation began.

"Shut up," Riley yelled, when her brothers and sisters continued talking. "Aaron's got an idea."

Aaron grinned at Riley and then looked at Sky. "My family owns a small cabin on the Shenandoah River. The house is small, but the amount of land surrounding it isn't. It's a very private place. If you and Teagan could get there undetected, you could finish your songs with nothing but the sound of the river to disturb you."

Sky was touched by the man's offer. "That's very generous of you," he said.

Aaron shrugged. "Teagan's been like a sister to me

for most of my life. There's nothing I'd like more than to hear one of her songs on the radio."

Teagan rose and kissed Aaron on the cheek. "That's a very sweet offer, Aaron."

Her words were calm, but Sky thought he detected a slight shaking in her hands. Was she afraid of being in a secluded place with him or afraid of leaving home? Until her father's words, he would have assumed the former even though she had his promise and he'd held true to it. Then he considered what he knew of Teagan. She did seem to be a creature of habit. She'd flat-out refused his offer to buy *Maybe Tomorrow* the first night they'd met, despite the fact she was a songwriter. Was her lack of ambition actually the symptom of a deeper fear? If so, what was she afraid of?

"So the trick is moving Teagan and Sky without the paparazzi following," Tris said.

"That's actually the easy part," Sky said. He'd dodged the press for years. "I've sort of adapted an idea I took from an old magician's trick. The one where you have to guess which cup the ball is under. Only we perform the trick with cars."

As he explained what they would need to do, Teagan drifted over to the window, covertly peeking down at the street below. She appeared to be genuinely disturbed by the paparazzi and he cursed himself for thrusting her into his crazy life.

Once the plan was laid, the family separated, each ready to do their part to help him escape with Teagan in tow. He and Teagan were charged with packing while the rest of the family went back downstairs. All of Sky's belongings had been retrieved by Ewan his first day in residence, so there would be no need to return to the hotel at all.

TEAGAN STOOD by her guitar and tried to figure out when she'd lost control of her life. A week ago, she'd thought she had her future sorted, her path laid. Now, as she bent to put her beloved guitar in its case, she realized everything was changing and she felt helpless to stop it.

"How was music class?" he asked.

"What?" She looked up, surprised by Sky's strange choice of conversation. They were about to try to pull the wool over the paparazzi's eyes and he was calmly asking about her music lesson with a bunch of preschoolers.

"Your class?" he repeated.

"It was fine."

He moved closer and she fought against the instinct to take a step back. She mentally shook herself for her foolishness. She wasn't afraid of Sky and yet she had to fight to hold her ground. His hands reached out to grip her waist loosely and she felt the familiar melting that occurred whenever he touched her. She was putty in his hands and she feared how far she'd go to keep him close. How much she'd sacrifice for him.

Except he's a rock star.

She'd been repeating the mantra for a week now and it hadn't helped. Fact was, she'd fallen head over heels for the man. He was charming and sexy and everything she'd ever hoped of finding in the man of her dreams.

He's a rock star. This isn't forever to him. Just a casual affair.

He leaned back a couple of inches, his eyes traveling down her body in a way she should have become accustomed to. The man had studied every square inch of her these past few days—clothed and unclothed. The tension in her body rose higher and for a moment, she considered slapping the smug, possessive smile that sprung to his lips.

"I bet every three-year-old boy in that preschool is in love with you."

"What?" she asked, taken aback again by his odd comment.

"Look at you. You're a beautiful, wild bird. A scarlet ibis. If I were a young boy, I'd want to capture you and put you in a cage, just so I could look at you and listen to you sing."

"If you were a boy?" she asked, her throat constricting on the words. His charm was lethal.

"I'm not a boy anymore. I'm a man and I know better."

"How so?"

"Your true beauty lies in your freedom. You sing to children and old people because it makes you happy. That's a precious gift you give. So," he paused and took a step back. For the first time since she'd met him, his face wasn't lined with laughter. It was serious, intense, and she felt herself becoming ensnared even tighter in his net. "I can't believe I'm doing this, but I'm releasing you from the bet."

"What?"

"I want you to write these songs with me, Teagan, but I don't want you to do it because your pop is pressuring you. Because your family is forcing a way of life on you that you may not want. Come with me and write them because it's what you want. If you don't want it, stay here. Stay with your family."

"I don't understand."

"I'm not about to yank you out of the safety of your home, the security of your family's arms, because of a bet. If you choose to come with me, you come with the knowledge that in all likelihood, your life is about to change. You have a very real talent and once it's discovered, I have no doubt the music world will be beating down your door for an original Teagan Collins song. I'd like to say your life will change for the better because of that exposure, but I'd be lying if I said it was all sunshine and roses. The worst part of it is standing outside on the sidewalk."

She looked toward the window, listening to the yells of the press and fans clamoring for a glimpse of Sky.

"But Teagan," Sky continued, "even dodging the paparazzi is worth it when you hear one of your songs on the radio or you stand on a stage before a packed stadium, everyone screaming and singing along to a song that you've written. It's just awesome. Amazing. God, I'd love to share that with you."

"Share it?"

"I was thinking perhaps we could turn *Maybe*

Tomorrow into a duet. It'd be a cool way to kick off your singing career," he said ruefully.

Her knees went weak at his words and for a moment, she felt as if she might faint. "Singing career? You've got it all figured out, don't you?"

Sky shrugged. "I'm just laying down your options."

"So you're giving me the choice?" she asked.

He nodded.

"And if I said I wanted to reject all those options, you would respect that?"

"Of course I would. You said yourself the night we met, you don't write songs for fame or fortune. You write them to share with the people you love. I respect that," he grinned, "even if I do think you're crazy."

She laughed sadly before sobering up. Too much was happening too fast and she found herself floundering in a sea of indecision. "What if I said I wanted to stay here? What would happen to the songs we've been working on?"

"I guess we'd have to decide what to do with them. They're your songs too, Ruby. I wouldn't steal them from you."

She turned away from him, her pulse fluttering at the sound of her pop's nickname in his sweet voice. Her mind and her heart were dragging her in a million different directions. If she went with him, her life would definitely change, but not necessarily in ways that would bother her. After spending the week working on the songs for his album, she'd been bitten by the bug. She wanted him to record the songs and she prayed he would find success in his solo career because he was truly talented and he deserved it.

But the idea of recording her own songs? It was a dream she'd never let her heart linger on, never considered a true possibility. Now Sky was offering her the chance of a lifetime and, as much as the idea terrified her, she knew she wouldn't say no.

Her deepest concerns about leaving centered not on the music, but on him. He'd released her from the contest because he thought she would hate a life in the spotlight. The fact was, she would hate a life without him more and the longer she stayed with him, the more painful it would be when they went their separate ways.

"If you're worried about being alone with me, gypsy…" he began, stepping closer, wrapping his arms around her waist from behind. She leaned back into his embrace, relishing the warmth of his body. "The promise still stands. I won't take anything you aren't willing to give."

Damn him, she thought. Couldn't he see? Didn't he understand? There was nothing she wouldn't give him. She closed her eyes, fighting to stem the tears threatening to fall.

"Well, then I suppose all that's left to do is pack. We have a grand escape to execute," she said, forcing the words through the tightness in her throat. She could do this. She had to.

"We?"

She turned and kissed him lightly on the cheek. "We have an album to finish. I don't renege on bets. Irish pride won't let me."

He grinned. "Is that right?"

"Well, that and *Maybe Tomorrow* would make an awesome duet."

He nodded and walked back to the bedroom to gather his things. She started to follow, surprised when Ewan returned to the apartment.

"Hey, Teagan," he said. "Wait up."

"What are you doing back here?"

"I wasn't sure I'd have a chance to talk to you alone before you left. I wanted to say, well, just be careful, sis."

She smiled at his kind words. "I've spent my life being the queen of careful, Ewan. It's time for me to spread my wings a bit. I mean, who would have imagined me doing something so adventurous?"

"Yeah, well, I'm happy for you—with the music and all. You're talented and you deserve this shot."

"But..." she said when she sensed he had more to say.

"But I'd hate to see you end up as one of Sky Mitchell's flavors of the month."

Her heart lurched at the thought. Had Ewan seen through her lame attempts at hiding her feelings? She studied his face and decided no. He was simply being her wonderful, loving, overprotective brother. She forced a grin to her lips. "No worries, Ewan. Given the fact Sky's taste usually runs from the exotic fashion model to the spicy Latina star, I don't think there's much chance he'll settle for plain old vanilla."

"Ah, Ruby," Ewan said. "With all those colorful clothes and feel-good songs of yours, I never saw you as vanilla. Rainbow sherbet, at least. Hell, maybe even bubble gum."

Teagan laughed. "Bubble gum. Yummy." She bent forward and kissed her brother on the cheek. He surprised her by grabbing her up in a big bear hug. "Thank you, Ewan."

He shrugged off her words, visibly embarrassed by her gratitude, and walked back downstairs. She looked around the apartment and took a deep breath. Regardless of how things ended in the cabin, she knew she was taking the first step toward leaving her childhood home. She'd expected to feel sad, scared, but instead she was overcome by a wave of positive, energized confidence.

I can do this.

Chapter Seven

They managed to give the paparazzi the slip in a car chase that would have made James Bond proud. Sky grinned when he recalled the enthusiasm of Teagan's brothers as they drove away from the pub. The Collins men would make great bodyguards. There didn't seem to be any challenge the men weren't up to when it came to tricking the cameramen. From bar brawls to racing through the busy city streets, they'd yet to let him down.

He unlocked the door to the small cabin Aaron's family owned. The man hadn't lied about the size. The entire structure was little more than a combination living room/ kitchen, a bedroom and a bathroom. Teagan peeked in each room then flashed him a relieved grin. "For a minute there I was worried we'd have to use an outhouse."

It was early November, but Virginia seemed to be experiencing an Indian summer. "At least there's a fireplace and large supply of wood if winter decides to kick in while we're here," he said.

"It's beautiful. The trees are still so colorful. Once we got away from the paparazzi and out in the country, it was a relaxing drive."

He agreed. Aaron had offered them the perfect escape and he'd have to find some way to properly thank the man. "Well," he said. "We've got enough groceries to last us awhile and I don't have to return to Baltimore until the week of Thanksgiving. That gives us three uninterrupted weeks to work our magic. You feel up to it?"

She smiled and nodded. "I was a bit nervous about leaving the apartment, but I have to admit this cabin seems to be the answer to a prayer. We won't have to deal with any of my brothers or sisters tromping through the room every few minutes to see how we're doing. I feel really good about this."

Her optimism was infectious and he shared her sentiment. They'd been granted a timeout, a brief respite from the real world where they could really focus on what mattered most to them—the music.

As soon as the thought passed through his mind, he realized that wasn't actually the reason he felt so happy. He was alone with Teagan for the first time in their short relationship. Though the promise still hovered between them, he looked forward to spending day after day, hour after hour getting to know her. There were large gaps in his knowledge of her that he was anxious to fill. Every step that brought them closer proved there were still miles separating them.

"I suppose we should get the groceries and our suitcases from the car." She headed for the door and he followed. For the next hour, they unpacked their clothing, food and instruments, chatting about this and that as they worked.

There was one bedroom in the cabin and it was furnished with only a queen-sized bed. They both avoided discussing the sleeping arrangements over dinner, opting to build a fire and begin work on *Maybe Tomorrow*. Teagan agreed to try to rewrite the song as a duet, but insisted if she didn't like the changes, he wouldn't record it—with or without her. They argued over pacing and some changes he wanted to make to the lyrics until nearly midnight, when he declared they should call it a night. They could finish the song and the fight in the morning. It was getting better, but Teagan was proving to be very stubborn about maintaining the acoustic guitar.

"Guess we should hit the hay. I'll sleep on the couch," he added, when he noticed apprehensiveness creep into her eyes as her gaze darted toward the bedroom.

"No," she said. "Don't be silly. We've been naked in each other's arms for a week. We can surely sleep in the same bed in our pajamas."

"I sleep naked," he said. It wasn't completely the truth, but the devil inside prodded him to push her. She'd annoyed him with her demands regarding the song and he was just petty enough to get a bit of revenge.

"Ewan must have been thrilled to see the back end of you as you left this afternoon then."

He laughed at her dry wit, reaching out to pull her close. "I want to sleep naked with you."

"I wear pajamas—tops and bottoms and underwear and socks. Sometimes even a bra."

"Liar," he teased.

"Well, I will be tonight."

He shook his head. "No. Tonight we're both sleeping naked."

She fell silent and he waited for her to deny his insane request. He was being demanding and he knew it.

She studied his face for a moment and he realized she was considering his words. Surely she wouldn't agree, would she? His heart raced at the idea of sleeping with a naked Teagan in his arms all night. Before they'd begun this conversation, he hadn't realized how much the idea appealed to him.

"Fine," she said so softly he wasn't sure she'd spoken at all. She walked toward the bedroom and he followed, wondering what sort of Pandora's box he'd just opened. Christ. He'd given his word not to have sex with her. He'd vowed to respect and protect her virginity. How the hell could he do that and still retain his sanity? He feared tonight would test the limits of his restraint more than he could withstand.

As they entered the bedroom, he stood in the doorway, spellbound as she slipped her sweater over her head as casually as if they'd done this every night for years. She removed her jeans and undergarments just as easily. He nearly bit his lower lip off when she bent over to pull down the quilt and sheets covering the bed. She crawled in, looking at him expectantly.

"Is something wrong?" she asked.

Holy hell no, he thought. For some reason, everything she was doing felt very, very right. "Lie on your stomach," he said.

She grinned at the commanding tone in his voice. "More games?"

He nodded, struggling to return her smile. He needed to keep things light, keep this thing growing between them casual. He could do casual. Fuck, casual was *all* he could do.

She rolled over, treating him to the image of her shapely, smooth back and firm buttocks. His cock rose from zero to sixty in under a second and he hastily pulled off his own clothing, haphazardly discarding them on the floor.

She laughed at his obvious eagerness. "We have all night," she reminded him.

"Don't remind me, gypsy. I'm a man on the edge here. I have too many things I want to do with you—*to* you."

"Sky, about the promise—" she started, but he cut her off.

"Say no if it goes too far. I swear to you I'll stop."

She didn't say anything and for a moment, he thought he saw the briefest glimpse of disappointment in her eyes. Did she *want* him to fuck her?

The moment the thought crossed his mind, he dismissed it. He wouldn't take her virginity. Not tonight. Not ever. Not even if she asked him to. This relationship—no, damn it, this *friendship*—was too new, too temporary for him to steal something so precious.

Cementing that thought in his mind, he formulated a plan. Their sexual games had been relatively vanilla since the night he'd introduced her to anal play, as he'd found himself satisfied to merely kiss and touch her. With other women, he'd always needed the roughness, the edge of pain. He'd loved pushing his bedmates to darker, wilder explorations. With Teagan, all of that stopped as he found he was genuinely content to merely hold her, caress her.

He crawled onto the bed and on top of her, caging her below his body. He felt her stiffen slightly when his cock brushed against her back. Maybe it was time to take them for a ride on the wild side. Maybe that would help him get on more even footing. He was skirting the edge of quicksand with her and he knew it.

He bent down and pushed her long, lovely hair over her shoulder. He pressed a kiss on the nape of her neck and as easily as that, she relaxed beneath him. Her calmness was short-lived when he guided his cock between her thighs. It rested against her pussy, the dampness there coating his throbbing flesh. He'd intended to leave it there for just a moment, but the second he found himself between her legs, all his good intentions—hell, all his common sense—flew out the window.

"Sky?"

"Shh. I promised," he said, the words getting

harder and harder to say. "Push your legs together. Just for a second. Hold my cock tight with just your thighs."

She obeyed, and for a moment he just savored the heat of her pussy against his hard-on. God, he closed his eyes and tried to remember why this was wrong. It felt so damn right. "You know how I rub your pussy, your clit with my fingers?"

She nodded.

"Tonight I'm going to do the same thing with my cock. We're going to go slow and easy and I swear to you, I won't put it inside you. I just wanna feel those sexy juices of yours coating me, covering me."

She trembled slightly and he grimaced. She wanted this as badly as he did, but he was a damn fool for initiating it. He was pushing himself to the brink of disaster but he didn't care. He wanted her right now more than he'd ever wanted another woman.

He lifted his ass, slowly pulling his cock along the firm clasp of her thighs. It wasn't as tight as he knew her pussy would be, but he didn't mind. The sensations of this pretend fuck were enough for now. They had to be.

He moved slowly up and down, absorbing her heat, the fluid flowing from her. He reached under her, using his fingers to tease her clit. She groaned at the first touch, her hips moving, reaching out for more. He felt the head of his cock bump against her entrance and for a moment, he swore it felt as if the devil himself was prodding him in the ass, daring him to just push it inside her a little. Just a little.

She whimpered beneath him and the sound awakened his senses. He pulled away quickly for fear her thrusting motion would send his cock inside her whether they wanted it or not.

"Hold still," he murmured, running his hand along his flesh, trying to find relief. He missed the hot clasp of her thighs the second he moved and felt his body overruling his mind once more. "Just let me fuck your legs. Let me pretend I'm inside that hot pussy of yours."

"Too good," she whispered. "I don't think I can take this, Sky. Not without wanting more. Wanting it all."

He closed his eyes and gritted his teeth, trying to remind himself of all the reasons why he shouldn't fuck her for real. Virgin. Casual sex. "God, gypsy. Please don't say that."

She closed her eyes and he could sense the effort it was taking for her to pull herself together. Her breathing was harsh, heavy, labored. "This is too hard. Too hard." A tear slid down her cheek.

Fuck. He'd been a fool to think he could start something like this and expect it to end innocently. What the hell was he doing? Maybe subconsciously he'd been hoping to tempt her. Hoping to drive her beyond her limits so she'd surrender her body, her virginity to him.

He took a deep, painful breath and pushed himself off her, moving to the side. Lying on his back, he covered his eyes with his arm and forced himself to breathe naturally. "I'm sorry," he said when he felt able to speak.

She didn't reply and he opened his eyes. She'd

covered herself with the blanket and he read the regret in her face.

"You don't have to be sorry, Sky. I seemed to have misplaced my 'no' there for a minute."

"I shouldn't have initiated that. I was tempting fate."

"Do you want to know why I've never slept with a man?" she asked.

He turned toward her, amazed by her sudden composure, her grace in light of the awkwardness of their situation. He'd been an asshole, but rather than being furious and telling him to get the hell out, she was giving him a reason, a rationale for her choices. She owed him nothing and yet, as always, she offered everything. "I assumed you were saving yourself for marriage."

She shook her head. "No, I'm not waiting for marriage."

He was surprised by her admission. "Then what?"

"Love, Sky. I'm waiting for love."

"There are all kinds of love, gypsy."

She smiled, her face serene, beautiful. She was a woman who knew what she wanted, who wouldn't compromise, regardless of his attempts to lead her astray. "I know that. I'm also old enough to know there are all kinds of things that disguise themselves as love. Infatuation, passion, fascination, lust. I've seen them all. Hell, I've felt them all, but they aren't what I want. What I deserve."

She was wrong. She deserved all those things…and love.

"So what do you want?" he asked, clearing his throat against the lump that had lodged there. He felt like a heel, an ass. She'd told him her limits and he'd pushed them, pushed *her*.

"Someone kind and thoughtful. Someone with a sense of humor who loves music. Someone who looks at my crazy clothes and doesn't seek to change my wardrobe but likes my silly style. Someone who thinks about me when he leaves and can't wait to come home to me each night. Someone who accepts me for who I am, freckles and all."

He nodded. "That doesn't seem too demanding."

She rolled her eyes. "Is that right? Then how come I'm twenty-six years old and I've never had sex? Apparently my sights are set way too high."

"No, they aren't. I'm going to let you in on a little secret. Men are idiots."

She laughed. "That's not exactly a secret, Sky."

He swatted her ass playfully. "You just haven't met the right guy yet, Ruby. When you do, you'll know, and he'll be the luckiest bastard on earth."

Her smile dimmed and he suspected he'd hurt her with his words. Dammit. She didn't think *he* could give her what she was looking for, did she? He was a fucked-up, driven rock star with too many aspirations and too much baggage. He wanted too much. Platinum albums, sold-out shows. He wanted to break every record a musician could break. He was too busy to fool around with an emotion as tricky, as complicated as true love.

He looked at her for a moment before closing his eyes against her beauty. So if all of that was right, then why did his heart ache with the thought that one day she would find the love she was looking for…with someone else? Was he jealous? Jealous of her? Or was he jealous of her dream? While Teagan knew exactly what she was looking for, what she deserved, he was sitting inside one lonely hotel room after another, hiding from the paparazzi, hiding from real life, content to drift in a sort of rock star Neverland.

"I think we should try to get some sleep," he said at last. "It's been a long day."

She leaned forward and kissed him lightly on the cheek. The touch was platonic, friendly, comforting.

"Good night, rock star."

"Night, gypsy."

SEVERAL DAYS PASSED as Teagan and Sky continued to work on their music. The paparazzi hadn't found them and for the first time in a long time, Sky was one-hundred-percent relaxed…and if he admitted it to himself, happy. As evening fell, they decided to call it a night on the songwriting. The days had begun to grow chillier, so he rose to throw some wood onto the fire he'd built earlier.

"I'm going to make some hot chocolate," she said. "You want some?"

Sky resumed his seat, toying with the guitar. "Yeah, that sounds pretty good. Marshmallows?"

She laughed. "Is there any other way to drink hot chocolate?"

He wiggled his eyebrows. "A woman after my own heart."

He strummed a few chords of one of The Universe's songs, the action relaxing after the long day spent working on their music. He listened as Teagan puttered around in the kitchen making their hot chocolate and he grinned at how comfortable their shacking-up together felt. She was easy to be around…when she wasn't driving him crazy over the songwriting. He chuckled and shook his head. Even fighting over lyrics and chords with her was fun.

He glanced up when she returned to the living room, startled when she cried out and spilled some of the steaming liquid on her hand.

"Ouch, dammit!" she said, turning to set the cups down so she could rub her wrist.

He rose quickly. "Are you okay? Here, let me see it." He grasped her hand in his, leading her back to the kitchen where he ran cold water from the faucet over the red skin.

"I-I saw a face," she stammered and he realized she was shaking—not from pain, but from fear.

"A face?"

"In the window, behind where you were sitting in the living room."

Sky felt the hair on the back of his neck prickle. Had they been found?

"I'll go look," he said, picking up a flashlight he'd noticed on the kitchen counter earlier. Teagan nodded as he left.

For several minutes he circled the cabin, but if

someone really had been there, they weren't now. When he came back inside, Teagan had cleaned up the hot chocolate and was sitting on the couch, calmer.

"Anything?" she asked.

He shook his head and she shrugged.

"I'm trying to figure out if I just imagined it," she said ruefully. "I'm a city girl through and through. I can't begin to tell you how much the silence of this place freaks me out sometimes."

He laughed at her admission as he locked the front door and joined her. He took her hand and looked at the small burn. The redness was already fading.

"We'll only be here for a couple weeks more and then you can go home to your incessant car horns, smoggy air and treeless existence."

"Thank God," she said with fake relief. "Sorry," she added sheepishly.

He leaned over and kissed her lightly. "No problem. It's been a damn long day. I think we should try to get some sleep."

She nodded as he led them to the bedroom. They changed into their pajamas, falling asleep within moments of lying down.

THE FIRST WEEK passed with a lazy, quiet sort of contentment. He and Teagan quickly fell into a comfortable pattern, working on their songs, eating, talking, taking long walks by the river. They'd continued to share the bed, but he hadn't initiated any more playing.

Touching her, kissing her had ceased to be a game to him and he found it impossible to think of their relationship as anything even remotely resembling a casual affair, so instead they'd become friends. Teagan seemed to take the newfound platonic nature of their relationship in stride. She was an amazing woman and he knew she would never pressure him for something he couldn't give.

He'd called Natalie and Rod a couple times to check in. His friends were relieved to know he'd escaped the paparazzi again and Natalie had expressed some jealousy over his vacation spot. She'd tried to invite herself to the cabin for a visit, but Sky had shot her down. He was barely able to sort out his confused feelings for Teagan. Natalie would take one look at him and realize he was a man on the edge. He'd expected his attraction to Teagan to wane or at the very least abate with the removal of their sex games. Unfortunately that plan had yet to pan out.

He'd also endured another rather painful conversation with Marty regarding his decision to leave the band. To say Marty wasn't taking the news well was the understatement of the century. Sky wasn't sure, but he thought the man had cried a bit at the end of the phone call.

By the end of their first week together, Sky realized his musical partnership with Teagan, the songs they were writing, could very well shoot him into another sphere professionally. He'd never been more proud of anything he'd done as a musician.

Of course, that point would be moot if he couldn't

get his computer working. He tapped a few more keys on the laptop, frustrated by the blue screen of death that stared at him.

"Fuck," he said, slamming his hand down on the worthless hunk of metal.

"Still not working?" she asked. He'd been trying to open a file for the last hour.

"No, the damn thing says I've got a virus. Christ, Teagan, all our songs are on this computer."

She shrugged, unconcerned, reaching for her notebook. "Guess you're just going to have to admit that sometimes the old ways really are better."

He laughed when she opened her beloved book, all the pages filled with their notes, their lyrics, their songs. He'd teased her relentlessly about writing out their music longhand when he had a software program that would make it easy.

He bowed to her. "Okay, I stand corrected on this one small point."

She shook her head. "You'll have to do a helluva lot better than that."

"I was wrong and you were right," he muttered, certain the grin on his face was giving away the fact that he didn't mind conceding the argument. She had their songs. The sheer relief of that fact pretty much ensured he'd say anything, do anything for her.

"That's better. I knew it was just a matter of time before I wore you down," she said, standing up and stretching. He was treated to a glimpse of her breasts outlined by her T-shirt and he felt his traitorous cock rise to the surface. Damn thing had been residing at half-mast for a week.

"I suppose we should get some sleep. I can barely keep my eyes open." She gestured to his computer. "You can keep beating on that piece of junk in the morning."

Sky nodded and yawned.

"The thing is toast," he agreed. He watched her walk to their bedroom, just as she had every night for a week—and he was struck by the realization that he wanted to make love to her.

Make love. Their bedroom.

Jesus.

She turned, confused when he failed to follow her. "Is something wrong?" she asked.

"No, I—I just want to make sure the door is locked. Go on. I'll be there in a minute."

She continued on and he walked to the mantel of the fireplace, gripping the wood tightly. He wanted to make love to Teagan. Sky Mitchell, king of the casual fuck, wanted to make love to her. He didn't do that. Hell, he wasn't sure he'd ever made love to Holly and they'd actually discussed marriage. Their sex life had been as volatile and heated as their romance. Love hadn't really figured into the equation.

This was wrong. Wrong, wrong, wrong. His head yelled at him to get a grip. He only *thought* he was in love with her. It was Teagan who was messing with his mind. She was a virgin. She was presenting a challenge he thought he'd been resisting. It was the old "wanting what you can't have" game. That had to be it. He wanted her because he couldn't have her. Teagan was saving herself for love, so he'd convinced himself he was in love with her.

Time to snap out of it, boy. You take her now, you're locking the ball and chain on your ankle and tossing away the key.

He took a couple deep breaths and walked to the front door. It was locked, just as he'd known it was. He reached over and pulled a blanket off the back of the couch, lying down on the lumpy cushions. He could resist her. He had to. He had his solo career, his future to think of.

Chapter Eight

Teagan woke up as the bright sun shone across the bed, blinding her for a moment. She glanced at the empty spot next to her. She and Sky had been at the cabin for over two weeks. Every night for the past week he'd elected to sleep on the couch and he hadn't touched her—not even a brushing glance—since then. She rubbed her eyes and yawned. She was tired of tossing and turning all night and confused as hell.

She'd assumed they'd continue their casual sex games at the cabin, but she sensed some part of Sky had shut down against her. She'd tried to fit into the role he seemed determined to place her in—that of a friend, a writing partner—hoping it would help to bring back the closeness they'd enjoyed in Baltimore. Despite her efforts to put him at ease, she felt like an outsider trying to peek into the windows of his soul. Problem was the blinds were drawn. He didn't want to pursue a long-term relationship—that much was clear.

Sky was only interested in casual sex and as soon as she'd made it clear that wasn't her style, he'd backed away. She could respect the honesty of his actions, even if they did slice through her like a knife.

She listened as he strummed a few chords of *Maybe Tomorrow*. Like their physical relationship, their musical partnership had disintegrated this past week into nothing but one argument followed by another. The notes, the melodies and harmonies, the words, had stopped coming and, as she lay on the bed staring at the ceiling, she sighed and wondered if he'd bother looking for her if she just stayed in bed all day. She was tired of forcing herself through the motions and she was homesick for her family.

She heard him hit a bad note and cuss, and then she heard the guitar hit the ground and the front door slam.

Great, another perfect day here in paradise.

She rose slowly and threw on her robe. She shuffled out to the living room where Sky's blanket lay twisted in knots at the end of the couch.

At least he isn't sleeping any better. The thought was petty and mean, but she didn't care.

She walked to the coffeepot in the kitchen and poured herself a cup of the strong brew Sky liked to drink. It was bitter on her tongue, but she needed any jolt of energy she could muster. Carrying her cup back to the couch, she set it beside the electric keyboard they'd set up their first night in the cabin. She turned it on and tapped a few notes.

Soon one of her favorite Billy Joel songs came to

her and she started playing the haunting, lonely melody. She closed her eyes and began to sing the words to *And So It Goes*, the lyrics and music matching her feelings. She'd driven Sky away. She'd given her true feelings away somehow and he'd shut down. She wasn't surprised by his response—he'd warned her repeatedly he was only interested in casual affairs, but the idea that she'd been such a coward tore at her insides. She'd tried for weeks to pretend nothing had changed for her, tried to convince him—and her—that she could handle the playing, the casual touches, the meaningless kisses. She'd lied to both of them. The song ended and she reached up to wipe away a tear.

"That was beautiful. One of my favorite songs."

Sky's voice from the doorway startled her. She tried to wipe her nose covertly on the sleeve of her robe. "Me too," she said, keeping her back to him.

"Teagan."

"Sky."

They'd both spoken at once and they laughed as she stood and turned to face him.

"Are you crying?" he asked.

She shook her head once then shrugged. Why hide it?

"Dammit," he mumbled miserably.

"I'm sorry," she said.

His face reflected his confusion. "Why?"

"I've put you in a position that really isn't fair to you. I told myself you were just a rock star, convinced myself you were a caricature and I've held on to the stereotypes attached to that persona like a damn life vest."

He took a step closer. "I think I did the same thing."

"How so?"

"There are some labels attached to virgins over the age of twenty."

She laughed. "I suppose there are. The thing is, Sky, you aren't just a rock star. You're so much more than that and despite my attempts to avoid it, I think… I mean, I know…I've fallen in love with you."

He opened his mouth to respond, but she waved his words away with her hand. "I don't expect you to say anything. You've told me from the beginning how you feel about serious relationships and I know you aren't looking for love. My feelings are my problem, not yours. I just wanted you to know how I feel. Maybe someday, somewhere down the road, you'll remember me and you'll be glad to know how much I cared about you."

SKY STARED AT HER, like the lost fool he was, his words failing him for the first time in his life. She'd done it, captured his heart, beaten down every crumbling structure he'd tried to erect against her. Worst part about it was, she wasn't asking for his love. She would never do that. She'd spent her life giving of herself and never once asking for anything in return. And, like an asshole, he'd taken everything he could grab for free with no regard for what it would do to her when he left. She was the bravest woman he'd ever met and with that realization the blinders fell away.

Unfortunately so did his words.

"I-I don't know what to say."

She nodded and he could see the effort it was taking her not to cry. "You don't have to say anything, Sky."

"Mitch."

"What?"

"My real name. It's Mitch Adams." He wasn't sure why he was offering her such a stupid fact at that moment, but all he could think was that he wanted her to know the real him. The normal man who wanted to live a normal life and love her until the day he died.

"It suits you."

He stepped forward, relieved when she didn't move away. Christ, she should be slapping him, hitting him, twisting his freaking earlobe after what he'd put her through the last couple of weeks. Reaching over, he placed his hands on her face, caressing her cheeks as he pulled her closer. She stood motionless as he bent to kiss her. As his lips touched hers, he knew all his excuses, his stupid ambitions paled in comparison to what this woman would mean to him. Be to him. He loved her.

For several moments, he tried to convey with his lips the feelings his screwed-up head was too afraid to confess. She pulled back.

"I can't be casual with you anymore," she whispered, her lips moving against his as she spoke the words, rife with pain.

He wrapped his arms around her shoulders and pulled her head to his chest. "There's nothing casual about this, gypsy. It's earth-shattering, traumatic, amazing, disturbing—perfect."

She laughed as she tightened her grip around his waist. "You realize those words don't really go together."

"I love you, Teagan. And believe me, in my screwed-up mind, every single one of those words applies."

She pushed away so that he could see her lovely freckled face, a single tear sliding down amongst the light brown dots. "Will you make love to me?"

"Forever," he vowed.

He took her hand and together they walked to the small bedroom. She led him to the bed again and he was amazed by the lack of haste. They undressed each other at a leisurely pace he could never have imagined. For weeks he'd burned for her, wanted until he thought he'd go mad with the craving. Now, as he slowly pulled the robe from her shoulders, he wanted nothing more than to savor every second, every sweet note. He wasn't merely writing a song with her. He was writing a symphony.

He pulled the T-shirt she wore over her head and smiled when the lovely pink flush he'd seen so many times painted her face and chest. "Still shy with me, Ruby?" he asked.

"It's hot in here," she said and he laughed at her obvious lie.

"Yeah, well, it's gonna get hotter."

She unbuttoned his shirt and he watched the slight quiver in her hands. Despite all they had done before, this was her first time and he wanted it to be special. Once she'd tackled the last button, he shrugged off the shirt before taking charge, pulling off his own shoes, socks and jeans.

Once they were completely naked, he stopped for a moment. He needed to catch his breath, calm his racing heart. "I love you," he murmured again and she grinned.

"Trying to convince me or you?" she teased.

"No convincing needed. I've acted like a fool these past two weeks, trying to cling to a lifestyle I can't stand. I want you beside me, Teagan, for as long as you'll stay."

She placed her fingers on his lips. "I believe you. You don't have to say anything. Just love me."

He kissed her again, using his lips, his hands to guide her back onto the bed. He covered her with his body and she groaned as his cock brushed against her pussy.

He moved his lips from her mouth to her cheeks and ears, working his way along her neck and down to her breasts at a leisurely pace. He wanted to taste every part of her, mark her as his. He drew quarter notes on her nipples with his tongue and she giggled at the tickling sensation until he wrapped his lips around the tight nub and sucked.

"God," she cried. Her legs wrapped around his waist and he was surprised by the strength of her need. "Inside me."

"Soon," he whispered, rubbing his lips against her fevered flesh. He pulled her legs away from him, drifting down her stomach with a long, luscious lick. When he got to her pussy, he was starving, ravenous. He'd intended for his teasing and continual soft touches to drive her insane, increase her desire, but in reality they had claimed *him*, made him a victim of his own tormenting, and he dove in with haste, tasting her sweet dew. She shook above him, her body in overdrive as he tormented her clit with his teeth before pushing his tongue inside her pussy. With his tongue, he mimicked the motions his cock was begging for until she jolted against him as if touched by a live wire. She screamed and he grinned at her incredible loss of inhibitions when in the throes of orgasm. She didn't hold anything back.

He crawled over her, impatient to find his own release. He placed his cock at the entrance to her body and cursed.

"Fuck. Condom." He moved rapidly to retrieve his wallet from the bedside table, pulling out the foil package and donning the damn rubber with shaking hands. He needed to be inside her. She laughed at his haste, using her own hands to still his as he slid the condom in place.

Once he was covered, he returned to her pussy, pushing the head in just an inch. He looked up at her face, determined to see every nuance of her expressions as he claimed her for the first time.

"You sure?" he asked, the words dragged from his

lips by some unforeseen force—his promise still hovering in the back of his mind.

"Positive." She wrapped her legs around his waist again and this time he let her drag him to heaven.

He pushed in slowly, consumed by the extreme heat, the almost unbearable tightness of her body. She held on to him, guiding him inside with a level of trust that nearly broke him. She was his to care for, to love, and once he was seated to the hilt, he made a silent vow to himself that he'd always protect her.

"Ready to rock and roll?" he asked lightly, hoping to distract her lest she was in pain.

She gave him a thoughtful, considering look for a moment. "Well, I guess. If we have to."

He laughed. "Hey, we could make this a slow country ballad. I just thought you might like the hard and fast beat of some heavy metal for a change." He punctuated the words "heavy metal" with a short, firm thrust of his cock and she moaned.

"Heavy metal," she gasped. "Definitely heavy metal."

"Good choice," he whispered as he placed a long, hard kiss on her lips. She wiggled impatiently after a few moments to let him know he was taking too long. He broke off the kiss and introduced her to his style of music—his thrusts hard and deep and strong. She screamed louder than the most adoring fan as she came, but he continued to play the song, to love her with everything in his body. When she came again, he was helpless to resist the pull of her pussy on his cock and he gave himself up to the music, to her.

For several moments they lay perfectly still, connected in ways Sky couldn't begin to fully appreciate or understand. All he knew was this was right. Very right.

Teagan's eyes were closed and he grinned as he studied her flushed face. She looked good with some color in her cheeks. He was surprised when her husky voice broke the silence.

"I can't wait to see what you do for an encore," she said.

The bed shook as they laughed, but soon the chuckles turned to kisses and the kisses gave way to touches.

It was an impressive encore. Even if he did say so himself.

TEAGAN OPENED HER EYES, surprised to find the room cast in darkness, only the soft glow of the moon providing a bit of light. She and Sky had spent hours in bed, exploring each other's bodies…and hearts. She still couldn't quite make herself believe his professions of love. It simply seemed too good to be true.

She'd spent too much of her life convinced she was happy and content, pushing away any feelings of loneliness with a vengeance. One day in Sky's arms, in his bed, had blown that misconception out of the water and she knew beyond a doubt she'd never truly known happiness until today. As far as first times went, she grinned with the certainty that she perhaps had just experienced the best one in the history of lost virginity.

"That's a cat who ate the canary look," Sky said, his voice husky, deep with sleep.

"Actually I think it would be more correct to just come out and say I look like a cat in heat," she joked.

Sky's eyes narrowed and she could see the hint of desire her words sparked. "I want you."

She grinned. He'd said the exact same three words at least four times during the day. "You're insatiable."

He shrugged. "Part and parcel of the image."

She laughed at his jest. "I better not show up in some tell-all book thirty years from now."

"No promises there," he said with a laugh. "Roll over onto your stomach."

"Why?"

"Because there's something I've wanted to do for two weeks and by God, I'm not waiting any longer."

She turned over, surprised when he quickly covered her, his chest pressed snugly to her back. His cock prodded at the vee of her legs and she started to open them until he used his knees to trap them together.

"Keep your legs closed."

She was instantly reminded of their first night in the cabin. The night they'd pushed their sex games too far.

He began to thrust between her legs, his thick, hard flesh rubbing against her clit until she thought she'd go mad. "Come inside me," she whispered.

"Not yet." He rose up on his knees and gripped her hips. "Raise your ass."

She obeyed, marveling at the fact she felt entirely comfortable despite being completely exposed to him.

"Remember that night in your bedroom?" he asked, his fingers slowly traveling from her pussy to her ass.

She recalled the way he'd fucked her ass with his fingers and she trembled.

"I can see you do," he said when she failed to respond.

He pushed the tip of one finger in her ass and she groaned.

"Do you like that?" he asked.

"You know I do," she replied, her words ending on a small squeal when he plunged his finger in deeper.

"I brought a toy with me. A sex toy."

She was beginning to become accustomed to his abrupt topic changes. "Why would you bring a sex toy here?"

He chuckled. "I'd intended to step our playing up a level or two."

"Or ten," she added.

"It's a slim vibrator," he said.

"Okay," she replied, dragging out the word, her body trembling at the thought of what he wanted to do with his toy. She may be newly initiated into sex, but she wasn't a fool.

"I want to use it on you." His finger moved slowly in and out of her tight portal as he spoke.

"Yeah, I didn't think it was for you," she said dryly.

"I want to put it in your ass, turn it on and then fuck your pussy."

She shivered in response. His dirty talk never failed to send a jolt of electricity through her. "Do it," she whispered, her body crying out for anything and everything he would teach her.

"Don't move a muscle," he said, punctuating the command with a quick, sharp slap on her rear end. She flinched at the unexpected smack. "God, I love your ass."

He got off the bed and she could hear him rummaging through one of the dresser drawers behind her. She remained on the bed, trying to calm the hormones raging through her body, trying to slow her rapid breathing.

He was back behind her in moments and she flinched again when something cold touched her ass.

"Lube," he said. "Thought it would make this easier. Christ, gypsy, I can't resist you. I can't stop wanting you. It's cruel of me to keep pushing you like this. I know you must be sore."

She halted his rambling with a soft, "Shhh." She turned to look over her shoulder and offered him a smile. "I love everything you do to me. In case you forgot, I have years and years to make up for."

"Well, then I guess we'd better get a move on." He added more lubrication to his finger, slowly working to stretch the tight muscles of her anus. Soon, she began to thrust toward his finger, trying to drive it in deeper, faster, and it was his turn to shush her. "Not this way, Teagan," he said as she clenched her fists into the pillow beneath her head. He pulled his finger out and she felt the tip of something hard pressing against her ass.

"Breathe out as I push it in. It's a bit bigger than my finger."

Slowly he worked the vibrator inside and she appreciated the patience and care he took as he initiated her into yet another wonderful, unexpected experience. Never in her wildest dreams would she have imagined allowing a man to play with her ass, but with Sky, nothing seemed too outrageous. When the vibrator was fully seated, he turned it on and she shuddered at the powerful stimulation the incredible toy provoked.

He tapped her ass lightly and touched her hips, moving her onto her side and then onto her back. She could see he'd donned a condom and she wrapped her feet around his waist, desperate to draw him inside her aching body. "I need you."

Sky smiled at her words. "I pray to God that never changes."

"It never will," she assured him as he placed his cock at the entrance to her pussy and gave her yet another taste of sweet heaven.

He halted for only a second when he'd reached the hilt before beginning a slow, steady pace, his movements thorough, almost reverent. She fought to restrain the climax hovering at the edges of her consciousness. He never failed to bring her to the brink in an instant. The vibrations of the toy in her ass combined with the thick, hard flesh of his cock piercing her was almost more than she could stand and she briefly wondered if anyone had ever perished from pleasure. His fingers grazed her ass and the vibrator began to move faster. Sky mimicked the action and she screamed as her climax broke free, dragging her into white-hot sensation. Somewhere in the distance, she thought she heard Sky cry out as well, felt his body tremble as completion claimed him.

Sky kissed her as she slowly regained her senses and she realized the vibrator in her ass was now off, though still inside her.

"Can I sleep now?" he asked slowly and she laughed.

"*You* jumped *me*, rock star."

"Mmm," he said as he rolled to the side. He quickly tossed the condom then returned, pulling her into a spooning position. His fingers teased the opening of her ass for just a moment before he dragged the toy out, setting it on the nightstand behind him. "That's right. I did. Guess I should warn you I intend to jump you again in about two hours."

"I'll consider myself warned."

"Good," he murmured and she could hear from his voice he was already drifting off to sleep.

"Very good," she whispered as she let the quiet night and soft sounds of Sky's breathing lull her back to sleep as well.

THE NEXT FEW days passed in relative contentment as Sky and Teagan drifted between the music they were writing and the love they were making. One mild evening, they took a long walk by the river, holding hands and talking about their dreams for the future. The songs they'd composed for the solo album were almost complete. The only song they couldn't seem to agree on was *Maybe Tomorrow*. They'd rephrased the lyrics for the duet, but while Teagan wanted the melody to remain light and unmarred by heavy accompaniments, Sky insisted it would sound better with a faster beat and the electric guitar.

While neither of them had said the words, The Universe's concert in Baltimore was looming in their future and they were worried about finishing the song in time. For some reason, the concert had become their unspoken deadline and they were feeling the anxiety of not meeting that goal.

As they returned to the cabin, Teagan was immediately struck by the feeling that something was wrong. Sky must have felt it too. He grasped her hand tighter, pulling her behind him as they climbed the stairs to the front door.

"Get behind me," he murmured.

"Sky?"

"The door is open," he said. "We closed it when we left. I know we did."

Teagan wished they'd thought to lock it as well. A few weeks in the country had undone twenty-six years of city living and they'd fallen into a foolish sense of security. They hadn't seen another living soul for weeks, so she supposed that feeling wasn't completely misplaced.

Sky slowly pushed the door open, peering inside.

Teagan glanced over his shoulder, taken aback by the sheer destruction that lay before them. Sky turned to look behind them at the surrounding woods and she could see he was torn between leaving her outside alone and bringing her into the house with him.

She took the decision out of his hands. She was terrified and she wasn't going anywhere without him. "I'll stay close," she murmured, releasing his hand and grabbing the material at the back of his shirt. He nodded and they entered the cabin slowly, cautiously. Whoever had destroyed the place was gone—that much was evident as they picked their way through the ruined furniture, checking in every room, every closet. When Sky felt sure they were alone in the cabin, he walked to the front door and locked it.

Teagan's shock and fear gave way to dismay when she spotted her beloved guitar in pieces on the floor by the fireplace.

"No!" she cried, dropping to her knees to pick up the ruined instrument.

"Oh, Teagan," Sky said, coming to stand behind her. "I'm so sorry, sweetie."

"It was my m-mother's," she said as the tears began to flow. "It was the only thing of hers I kept."

He knelt beside her and she could see he was as distraught by her loss as she was. "I didn't know." He reached out and held her as she cried. Seeing her beloved instrument—her only physical link to her mother—shattered, triggered all the old grief at her mother's death. Sky held her throughout and she clung to him, desperately trying to pull his strength around her. She'd never felt quite so devastated.

After several long minutes, she pulled away.

"Sorry," she said. "Fell apart, didn't I?"

"Don't apologize for that, Teagan. Someone's going to be sorry for this, but it's not going to be you." As he spoke, he looked around the room and she could see the deep-seated anger the destruction had planted in him. "Someone clearly knows I'm here," he said at last.

She nodded. It did appear their private Garden of Eden had been discovered. "Why would someone want to trash the place?"

Sky pointed to his laptop computer. Amongst the chaos it lay untouched, almost as if someone had known it was useless, destroyed. "I have a suspicion," he said.

"Your solo career?"

"I didn't really put it together until tonight, but the paparazzi's pursuit of me lately has been a bit rabid, even for them."

"You think someone was siccing them on you to keep you from writing your songs."

He shrugged. "I suppose that part could just be a coincidence, but I don't think so. I believe someone is sending a pretty obvious message about wanting to see my solo career fail before it even starts. Leaking my cell phone number to the press, uploading a virus to my computer. I think you really did see a face in the window that night."

"Who would do all that?" she asked and he laughed mirthlessly.

"Shit, it might be easier to make a list of people who want me to succeed." He shrugged. "I think it's safe to say my manager and the other members of The Universe probably aren't exactly my biggest supporters right now."

"What about your record company?"

Sky shook his head. "I don't think they care one way or the other. I haven't said I'm leaving my label, just the band."

"I assume Marty told the other band members you're leaving."

Sky nodded. "He did. I don't think any of them were particularly surprised. I've been hinting around for months. I heard a rumor once that they'd actually made a list of singers who could replace me. I don't know if that was true, but—"

"The problem with all of this is that The Universe and Marty don't know we're here," she interjected.

He sighed heavily and she could see that realization had already occurred to him. "I know, gypsy, but I don't want to consider the people on the list who *do* know we're here. I don't want to think that any of them could have done this."

She closed her eyes wearily. Her family and Aaron knew they were here. She couldn't for a moment conceive of any of them doing such a thing. For one thing, Teagan's dreams for a successful music career were on that laptop too. None of her siblings would destroy that…

Or their mother's guitar.

"It wasn't my family," she said quietly, steeling

herself for the onslaught the comment might provoke. She recalled the fact that Sky had suspected someone in her family of tipping off the paparazzi back in Baltimore.

"I know," he said quietly.

"You do?"

Sky's thoughts echoed her own. "Your family would never wreck your chance at becoming a songwriter, a musician. Besides, they have nothing to gain if my solo career doesn't take off and you have everything to lose."

"So…" she started, unwilling to fill in the blanks of their very short list.

"So," he finished sadly, "it was Rod or Natalie."

Her heart broke as he said the words and she could see the pain that thought was causing him. While she'd sat on the floor mourning the loss of her beloved guitar, Sky had been grieving over the end of a lifelong friendship. He'd been betrayed.

"What do we do now?" she asked.

She watched as he seemed to force himself to switch gears and she saw Sky the Plotter emerge. She'd been impressed by his quick thinking in the closet at the pub, but that seemed nothing compared to his scheming now. Anger was driving him and he wouldn't rest until he'd discovered the truth.

"Do you still have the notebook? The one with all our songs?" he asked.

She leaned over to retrieve the small bag she'd carried with them on their walk. "Yes, it's in here."

"It's probably a given whoever did this was looking for them."

"So we'll keep the songs safe. Sleep with them under our pillow," she said.

"I love you," he said, leaning forward to kiss her.

"Protecting the songs only solves one part of our problem," she said as they broke apart.

"I know. For the rest, I think we need to call in the reinforcements."

"Reinforcements?" she asked.

"Yep, I'm afraid we're going to have to recruit that group of wild Irish you call a family."

Chapter Nine

The night of The Universe's concert arrived too quickly for Teagan as she and Sky had spent most of the days since the break-in making plans to trap Sky's betrayer. They'd snuck back into the city yesterday morning and filled her family in on their plans. Teagan grinned as she recalled their enthusiasm at helping to catch the person who'd betrayed Sky. It occurred to her that her crazy siblings were suddenly counting Sky as one of them and she could see the delight on Sky's face when he realized the same thing.

As she stood backstage with Sky, she felt the exhilaration and energy he'd tried to describe to her on the way here. Words couldn't express the level of excitement coursing through her as she watched stagehands and sound technicians running through their checks. She, Keira, Riley, Pop, Sean and Will had ridden to the arena in a limousine—Teagan's first time in that kind of vehicle. Tristan and Ewan were escorted in by the police in the car behind them. Sky had hired Aaron for the night to work as his personal bodyguard prior to and following the show.

She could understand Sky's addiction to performing at this level. The idea of twelve thousand screaming fans all paying to come hear his music—

"Nervous?" Sky asked, his arm snaking its way around her waist.

She shook her head. "No, why should I be? You're the one who has to go out on the stage."

She felt his lips curl into a grin at the nape of her neck. "I was talking about the Sherlock Holmes-style trap we're about to spring."

She shook her head. She'd been so lost in the powerful pull of the stage, she'd forgotten what had to happen before Sky stepped out to perform.

He turned her to face him, touching her cheek softly. "It's like magic, isn't it?"

She nodded, pleased that he always seemed to be able to read her mind. She'd never met anyone with whom she felt so closely linked. "I understand why you feel compelled to succeed. I don't think I could perform at this level without wanting more. It's quite heady, wonderful."

"One day those fans will be filling the seats to see you."

She laughed and scoffed. "I doubt that, but it's a nice dream."

He looked as if he wanted to continue the argument, but Ewan walked up. "The key players are in place. You guys ready to do this thing?"

"Jeez, Ewan. You sound like Bruce Willis in one of those *Die Hard* movies," she teased.

Ewan grinned and she read the utter excitement on his face. She knew that tonight, despite everything they were facing, was a night none of her siblings would ever forget. They were backstage at the final concert of The Universe. History was writing itself before their eyes and they were there—up close and personal.

"Natalie, Marty, Rod and the rest of The Universe are all waiting for you in your dressing room," Ewan said to Sky. "If we're gonna spring this trap, the time is now."

Sky grasped Teagan's hand and she squeezed it for encouragement as she watched a grim expression claim his handsome features. Tonight would not be easy for Sky on many levels. He was about to discover which of his friends had betrayed him and a big chapter of his life was about to close. When he walked off that stage at the end of the night, he would be facing an uncertain future. While she had no doubts about his success, she knew Sky was worried he'd made the wrong decision, scared he'd fail.

"Ready?" he asked as they reached the door to his dressing room. She nodded as Ewan peeled away, drifting down the hallway to meet up with the rest of the Collins clan. The chatter in the room died down at their arrival and Sky thanked all of them for taking a few minutes to join him.

He stepped forward, pulling her with him. "I wanted to formally introduce you all to Teagan Collins. Teagan has been helping me write the songs for my solo album." No one made a sound or twitched a muscle. Teagan watched Rod and Natalie closely as Sky continued to speak. "I know by now, you all know of my intention to leave The Universe. I can't tell you how sad I'm going to be to walk off that stage tonight knowing it's the last time we'll ever be together."

The drummer of the band, Spike, nodded, smiling sadly.

"Been a great ride," Joe Roxy, the bass player, said.

"Been a fucking awesome ride," Spike added.

"I know Marty wanted to make a formal announcement about our disbanding tomorrow, but I feel like we owe it to our fans to let them know tonight. Let them know that they're seeing something a hell of a lot more special than just a rock concert," Sky said. The band members clearly agreed and Teagan was touched by how much they respected Sky's decision and how much he cared about them.

"Sky," Marty said. Teagan thought the red-faced, stressed-out man appeared to be on the verge of a coronary. His skin was mottled, sweaty, and she could read definite fury in his eyes. "We agreed to make the announcement tomorrow at a press conference. Tonight isn't a good time."

Sky shrugged. "I don't agree. In fact, if the guys don't mind, I'd like to make the announcement toward the end of the second set and then wrap the set up with a song Teagan and I wrote for the solo album. Sort of kick off my new beginning in style."

Marty's chest rose and fell rapidly, but Rod and

Natalie didn't react. Teagan thought Natalie even looked a bit bored.

"Is that okay, guys?" Sky asked the band.

"Fuck yeah!" Spike said. "We're gonna rock this motherfucking arena and then we're gonna get some major pussy."

Sky laughed. He'd warned Teagan about the drummer's fondness for the F word and sex. He'd commented on more than one occasion that Spike's entire world revolved around three sticks—the two in his hands and the one in his pants.

Marty stepped forward, his voice eerily calm. "I wish you would change your mind about this, Sky."

Sky shook his head. "My mind is made up."

"So be it," the manager said. And he stormed out of the room.

The other band mates filed out as well after exchanging high fives and hugs with Sky before returning to their own dressing rooms. Natalie was the next to leave, hugging Sky and telling Teagan she was pleased to finally meet the hippie who'd stolen her buddy's heart. Teagan liked the woman instantly and secretly prayed Natalie wasn't the betrayer.

Rod came up next, shaking his head. "So you're really gonna do it," he said. "Gonna fly solo."

Sky put his arm around Teagan and said, "Well, not completely solo."

Rod eyed her with interest, and then grinned. Teagan thought his smile didn't quite reach his eyes. "I'm happy for you, man. Really happy. Break a leg out there."

Sky shook Rod's hand and Teagan could see Rod's surprise at the formality of the gesture. She watched the man mentally shrug and leave.

"Let the games begin," Sky muttered.

They had set it up so that each of Teagan's siblings followed a different suspect. If the villain was desperate enough, they figured they'd make a strike to stop Sky's announcement prior to the concert.

"Aaron's outside," she said, having caught a glimpse of Riley's best friend upon Rod's departure.

Sky nodded. "Guess we'll see how badly someone wants to stop me."

Teagan knew Sky was praying whoever was setting him up for failure would simply give up the effort. Problem with that ending was, they may very well never know who'd destroyed the cabin and set the paparazzi loose on Sky.

"Well, I better get out of here," she said, kissing him lightly on the cheek.

Sky frowned. "Teagan—" he began, but she cut him off with a wave of her hand.

"I'm following Marty, Sky, and that's all there is to it."

He shook his head, but she refused to be baited into the same argument they'd fought all day. She'd insisted on trailing Sky's manager while Ewan shadowed Natalie and Tris took Rod. Pop, Keira, Sean and Will were all keeping an eye on the members of The Universe even though she knew Sky didn't suspect any of his former band mates.

"This is a mistake," he said, his words familiar given the fact he'd repeated them to her all day.

"I want to help you figure out who's doing this. Besides, in case you've forgotten, the bastard broke my mother's guitar."

"I don't like the idea of you being in danger."

"I'll be surrounded by other people. It's a madhouse out there. A hub of activity with everyone scurrying around to get ready for the concert. I'll be fine."

Sky sighed. "Be careful."

"You too," she whispered, kissing him quickly once more before leaving the room.

Teagan panicked for a few minutes as she struggled to find her prey, not breathing easily until she caught up to him at the far end of the stage. He was on the phone and fortunately he had his back to her. She hid behind one of the long velvet curtains, trying to hear what he was saying.

"I don't give a fuck what you have to do," Marty said. There was silence and Teagan prayed he would say the name of the person he was talking to.

"He can't go on that stage tonight. Period. We're moving up the time schedule."

She was torn between listening to the rest of the conversation and rushing back to warn Sky. Apparently he was in more danger than they realized. Marty sounded like a man on the edge and she suspected there was very little he wouldn't stoop to in his desire to keep Sky in the band.

A stagehand bumped into her from behind. "Oh excuse me," the man said. "I didn't see you there."

Marty turned at the sound of voices and spotted her watching him. His eyes narrowed menacingly and she decided flight was definitely a good idea. She turned quickly to run, but Marty rushed over and grabbed her arm when she found herself blocked in by the bulky piece of equipment the stagehand was carrying.

"What's your hurry, Teagan?" Marty asked. "We haven't had time to get to know each other. I hear you're an excellent songwriter. Have you considered hiring a manager?" She knew the manager's words were for the benefit of the stagehand, who grinned at her and nodded. No doubt he thought today was her lucky day. The stagehand didn't notice the death grip Marty had on her upper arm. "Why don't we head over to Sky's dressing room and discuss it?"

He pushed her forward roughly as the stagehand continued on in the opposite direction. "Sky's dressing room is on the other side of the arena," she said, trying to dislodge his painful grip.

"So it is," Marty said, not altering his course. "I've changed my mind. It's more private on this side of the stage. In fact, we might not run into another living soul who could interrupt us."

"What are you going to do?" Teagan asked as Marty opened a props closet and shoved her inside. Her hands began to shake when he followed her inside and shut the door.

"No," he said menacingly. "I think I'll tell you what

I'm *not* going to do. I'm not going to watch my nest egg float away because some sixties reject turned his head."

Teagan narrowed her eyes at his insult. She wasn't a reject. "Maybe if you weren't acting like such a prick, you could have represented your *nest egg's* new career," she said, punctuating "nest egg's" with air quotes.

"My contract is with the band and it's not up for another three years," he said, as if she was stupid. "Even if Sky leaves them, I have to stay. What the fuck good is The Universe without Sky Mitchell? Worst part is, those fucking idiot band mates of his think they can still succeed without him and have no intention of calling it quits. I'm trapped in a losing proposition. I need more time," he said, half to himself.

Teagan glanced at her watch. Whoever Marty had been talking to on the phone was clearly on the move. She looked around the room, trying to find a way out before Marty decided she was an expendable problem.

Her prayers were answered when Marty's cell phone rang. The unexpected sound and Marty's scrambling to pull the thing out of his pocket gave Teagan the few seconds she needed.

She picked up the microphone stand to her left and hit him on the shoulder—hard—before he could react.

The force knocked him off balance and she used the momentum to push him to the ground, where he landed in a pile of tulle. As he struggled to stand up, she dashed out the door, using the stand to jam the doorknob.

Run! she told herself, as she dashed around stagehands and sets. Too much time had passed. She had to get to Sky before it was too late.

———

SKY PACED the small area of his dressing room, worrying about Teagan, her family, the concert. Hell, he was worried about everything and feeling pretty damn useless. He shouldn't have let Teagan go after Marty. While the man was a blustering oaf, Sky prayed he hadn't underestimated his manager's annoyance at his leaving the band.

"Hey."

He was startled by Rod's voice at the door. "Hey, Rod," he said, glancing behind his friend to see where Aaron was.

"Your new bodyguard got called away. Some sort of police emergency."

Sky nodded, his entire body on alert. "What's up?"

Rod shrugged, entering the room before closing and locking the door behind him. Unbeknownst to his friend, they'd disengaged the locks earlier in the afternoon. While the door appeared to be locked, Sky knew it wasn't.

"I've been thinking about your decision to leave The Universe, talking to Marty. You know you're taking a pretty big risk, right?"

Sky nodded numbly. It was Rod.

Images flashed before his eyes—the two of them playing on the same Little League team, double-dating to school dances. Rod had sold him out. "Part of the business," he said, proud of the strength in his voice in light of the fact he felt as if the breath had been knocked out of him.

"I just don't understand it, Sky. I mean, you and The Universe are rocking the charts. You don't have any of those fucked-up problems other rock groups do. None of you are addicted to drugs, you don't have epic battles. You've got the real deal here. The good life."

"It is a good life, Rod. Thing is, I want a great life."

Rod shook his head, frustration and anger building in his face. "You know, that's the problem with you, Mitch. You're never satisfied. You've freaking got every goddamn thing in the world and you still want more."

Sky shook his head slowly, wondering where his friend's words were coming from. They'd spent their entire childhood competing against all comers to be the best. Rod was as competitive and driven as he was. Rod had sold more houses during his first year as a real estate agent than his colleagues had in a decade. He was the youngest person to ever make partner in his real estate firm.

"I thought you understood my decision," Sky said. His friend was pacing the room and Sky could tell he was fighting with himself over something. Sky watched his friend's hand drift to the pocket of his jacket for the third time. What the fuck was in his coat? Where was Aaron?

"Well, I don't. I don't understand and I think maybe you should reconsider."

"It's a little late for that," Sky said.

"No, it's not." Rod's hand slipped into his pocket and this time he latched on to whatever was there.

At the same time, the dressing room door flew open and a breathless Teagan rushed in.

"Sky, it's Marty! He'd got somebody working for—"

"Teagan!" Sky yelled, but it was too late. Rod grabbed her from behind and, with horror, Sky learned what his friend had been hiding.

Rod pressed a syringe against Teagan's throat.

"Well, well, well. Look who's here," Rod said. Sky could see his grip on Teagan tighten as her face contorted with pain…and fear.

"What are you doing, Rod?" he asked softly.

"I'm finishing a job. A job that will put me on easy street."

"What job?" Sky asked, trying to figure out how the hell he could get Teagan out of his friend's grasp.

"I've got some debts, Mitch. You said it yourself. The economy sucks. The housing market is in the gutter."

"I said I would loan you money. The offer still stands. Just take that," he motioned to the needle, "away from her neck."

Rod grinned and for a moment, Sky was struck by the fact that his friend most definitely wasn't in his right mind. "It's heroin. Enough to send her into overdose. Maybe even enough to kill her."

"What the hell are you doing with heroin?"

"Marty doesn't want you to leave The Universe," Teagan said. Sky's gaze flew to her pale face. She was scared to death and yet he saw the vein of strength she'd proven time and again she possessed. "His contract is with the band, not you. If you leave, he's pretty much ruined."

"You've got a smart girlfriend here, Mitch."

Teagan flinched as Rod pulled her more tightly against him.

"It was you," Sky said. "You've been feeding the paparazzi my whereabouts. You know how much they drive me nuts."

"I thought they'd distract you from writing the songs for that solo album."

"I suppose it was you who broke into the cabin and destroyed Teagan's guitar. It was your face she saw in the window that night."

Rod nodded, his eyes blinking rapidly. Sky worried his friend would unravel completely and hurt Teagan before they could find a way out of this predicament.

"I had to do it," Rod said, his voice strained. "Marty and I have a vested interest in seeing the band stay together."

Sky was confused. "I understand Marty's interest, but not yours. What is Marty to you?"

"Who do you think I owe the money too, Mitch? Marty. I owe *him*. Only now he doesn't want his fucking money back. He wants his payment in blood."

"What are the debts from?" Sky asked, a terrible realization crashing down on him.

Rod shrugged.

"Where did you get the heroin?"

At his second question, Rod's eyes drifted down to the needle and, for a moment, Sky was struck with the impression that his friend wished the syringe was piercing his own skin.

"When did you start doing drugs?" Sky asked, wondering how he could have missed such an obvious truth.

"Marty's a very accommodating manager. Man knows how to throw an after-concert party. Shame you never saw fit to partake. He could have kept you in line a helluva lot easier," Rod sneered.

A bell rang, warning the band members that the concert was set to begin in five minutes. It stirred Rod to action and he pulled Teagan toward the wall behind him. "So here's how this is gonna go down," he started. "You're gonna go out there and play your fucking heart out on that stage. Never at any point are you to mention leaving the band or going solo. Your girlfriend and I will be watching from the sidelines. You say anything about leaving and I pump this lethal dose of drugs into her and you can watch her die. Keep your mouth *shut*."

"So that takes care of tonight," Sky said. "You can't hold a syringe to Teagan's neck for the next ten years."

"I can hold it there long enough for you to re-sign with The Universe. Marty has the contract with him. Have to tell you, your girlfriend saved you from a pretty embarrassing overdose, Mitch. I don't imagine too many labels would have been anxious to sign a singer with a known addiction to heroin."

So that was the original plan. Pump him full of drugs and ruin his reputation. Make staying with The Universe seem like the only choice left.

A voice from the hallway called out, "Show time."

Sky started walking to the door, wincing when Rod pressed the tip of the needle into Teagan's neck. "No fast moves," his friend warned. "Just walk normally and don't look back."

Sky nodded, his fists balling up in anticipation of the moment his friend let go of Teagan. He'd kill the asshole for even daring to threaten her life. He opened the door and stepped into the hallway. No one was in sight so he walked in the direction of the stage. The roar of the twelve thousand fans packing the crowded arena was almost deafening.

The stage manager came into view ahead and Sky wondered if Rod had seen the other person. A scuffling noise behind him sent him spinning around.

He found Rod on the floor on his knees, Teagan twisting the man's earlobe with one hand while trying to hold back the other hand with the syringe.

Sky ran toward them, grasping Rod's hand a split second before the needle punctured Teagan's chest. He heard his friend's wrist snap as he twisted it.

As easily as that, the fight seemed to leave Rod. He dropped back onto the floor, cradling his broken wrist and watching as Sky stepped on the syringe, breaking the vial, the lethal liquid pooling on the concrete.

"No!" Rod gasped and Sky saw how deep-seated his friend's addiction was.

Teagan had slunk down to the floor, her back to the wall, and he realized the fear and exertion had given way to genuine shock.

"Teagan," he said, rushing over to her as several

members of the Collins family and the stage manager ran toward them. He dropped down beside her, pulling her into his arms as she began to shake. "Did he inject you?" Her face was even paler than usual and he suddenly worried Rod had managed to shoot some of the heroin into her system.

"No," she whispered.

Tris and Will hurried toward them. "Is she hurt?" Tris asked, concern in his voice.

"I'm fine," Teagan said. "Just had the shit scared out of me. Give me a minute."

Aaron and Sean showed up next, dragging Marty with them. Aaron had cuffed the cussing manager. "We found this guy trapped in a closet. He wants to press charges against Teagan for assault."

"I'll have your badge for this!" Marty yelled.

"Figured he must've been involved when he said she was the one who hit him," Aaron said.

"He and Rod were in cahoots, hoping to use a heroin overdose and a ruined reputation to keep me with The Universe," Sky said, gesturing to the crushed syringe.

Aaron bent down and carefully picked up the broken needle with a handkerchief.

As Sky explained what had happened in the dressing room, he tilted Teagan's head, touching the sore spot where the needle had pierced her skin. "You should see a doctor," he murmured.

"And miss the biggest concert of the year? No way." She smiled and Sky was happy to see she'd appeared to regain some of her usual spunk and spirit.

"There's no way I can go on now," he said. He was worried sick about her and there were all the loose ends to tie up in regards to Marty and Rod.

"Why not?" she asked. She took his face in her hands, capturing his gaze. "All of this will keep for a couple of hours. Listen, Sky. Listen to your fans. They want you."

He noticed for the first time since reentering the dressing room the chanting that was pounding through the arena, the sound deafening now that the beating of his heart had died down. Thousands of people were screaming his name.

"Sky. Sky. Sky."

Teagan kissed him lightly. "Go sing, Mitch. Knock 'em dead."

He grinned and nodded. Rising slowly, he pulled her to her feet and gestured for the stage manager to introduce the band.

Teagan walked with him to the wings and he found himself hesitant to release her hand. "Kiss for luck?" he asked, feeling as if he were about to perform his first show. Teagan had done that for him. She'd taken his boring world and breathed new life into it. She'd taken him from black and white to Technicolor.

"You've never needed luck," she whispered. "You have the luck of the Irish."

He shook his head. "My Irish luck didn't start until the day you lost that singing contest."

She laughed. "I let you win. Didn't want to bruise your fragile ego."

"Ladies and gentlemen," a voice called out over the

loudspeaker. The roar of the crowd grew louder and Sky realized any response he made to her comment would be lost in the din. "The Universe!"

He stole one more hard, fast kiss and stepped out onto the stage.

Chapter Ten

Teagan watched the show from the wings with her brothers and sisters. They were singing along and dancing and she honestly couldn't remember when she'd had more fun with her family. The night, which had started out so terrible, had turned out to be one of the best of her life.

As the second set started to wind down, Sky stepped to the microphone and announced his decision to leave The Universe. His speech was brief, but poignant and beautiful, and she felt a tear spring to her eye when he announced that he was donating his portion of the concert proceeds to her nursing home. She knew in that moment she would love Sky Mitchell until the day she died.

He walked back to the guitar racks and, to her surprise, picked up an acoustic guitar. He looked over at her as he returned to the microphone. "I've recently acquired a new writing partner. A brilliant musician and talented songwriter. She helped me write the songs for my forthcoming solo album and I'd like to introduce you to her and her song, *Maybe Tomorrow*."

Teagan's mouth fell open as he turned and held his hand out in her direction. "Ladies and gentlemen, Teagan Collins," he said.

She stood spellbound for a full minute before she became aware of Riley shoving her none too gently onto the stage. The applause as she crossed the stage was polite and she wondered when Sky had suddenly gotten so far away from her. She'd thought him only a few feet away while he was performing, but now as she walked, she realized the stage stretched on for miles and miles. The bass player brought up two stools and Sky handed her a microphone.

She shook her head slightly, leaning forward a bit. "We didn't finish this song."

"Yes, we did," he said. He strummed the first few bars and she realized he was conceding the argument, performing the song her way. He was leaving his comfort zone and stretching his wings. As he sang the first verse, she knew she'd never heard a more beautiful song. Somehow she found the courage and strength to lift the microphone and she joined him on the chorus before singing her verse. The crowd disappeared as they sang and Teagan was reminded of the night of the contest. The first time she'd ever shared a stage. Sky had been her first in so many ways and she vowed he would be her last as well.

As the final note faded, the crowd went crazy, cheering and screaming—not just Sky's name, but hers as well. He'd given her the dream she'd been afraid to dream.

She and Sky bowed. He announced there would be a short break, after which The Universe would perform their last set and, no doubt, an encore. As enthusiastic as this crowd was, they might need to do a few encores.

As they stepped off the stage, Teagan's family was there, hugging her, offering their congratulations. Teagan thought for a moment she saw Riley wipe away a tear, but she was certain she must have imagined it. Pop was the last to step forward and he was openly crying. "I've never been more proud," he said as he placed a kiss on the top of her head. "You looked and sounded just like your mother out there. I'm going to miss hearing you sing at the pub every week, Ruby, but you were always too good to stay with us. You were born for this, for more."

She hugged her pop tightly before he released her, placing her hand in Sky's. "Take care of her, son."

Sky nodded solemnly. He looked at her, tilting his head to the side. "Can I talk to you for a minute? Alone?"

"Of course."

He took her back to his dressing room and she grinned when he took a chair from the corner and propped it under the doorknob.

"What are you up to? You do realize it's only a short break."

"I don't give a shit," he said. He kissed her voraciously, hard. "Lift up that skirt and bend over the dressing table."

"Sky," she said, uncertain she'd ever seen him so intense, so driven.

"I need you, gypsy. Now. Seeing Rod holding that needle to your throat. Hearing you sing on that stage. Jesus, if I don't fuck you right now, I swear to God I'll die."

She started to laugh, but he looked like he was in agony and she realized he was being completely serious. She walked to the table, not surprised to find him right on her heels. She lifted her skirt, pulling down her panties as he fumbled with the condom. He was inside her before she'd finished bending over. The sigh that escaped his lips seemed to be pulled from the depths of his chest. "This won't take long. I can't—I won't be able to—"

"Shhh," she said. "Just fuck me, Sky."

He moved inside her, fast and furious, pumping into her hungry pussy like a drowning man swimming for land. She looked up, thrilled to realize she could see his face in the mirror in front of her. His face reflected his pleasure at taking her, the pain of his intense desire.

"Harder," she urged as his eyes met hers in the mirror. He reached around her, pinching her nipples through her shirt, his hips thrusting faster.

"God, you're gorgeous," he said and she looked at her own reflection, shocked by the woman looking back at her. She almost didn't recognize the flushed face, heavy-lidded eyes, kiss-swollen lips. She moaned as he moved deeper and the sound seemed to break something inside him.

"Fuck. It's not enough." He pulled out, spinning

her in his arms and lifting her onto the table. "I have to kiss you."

He pulled her ass to the edge, pushed his cock inside and devoured her lips, swallowing her cries as he drove her to the heights of passion. She reached her climax just seconds before him and only a minute before the stage manager knocked on the door to announce the beginning of the third set.

He pulled her to his chest, stroking her hair gently. His next kiss was soft, almost apologetic. "Teagan, I'm—"

She stopped his words with a finger on his lips. She gave him a mischievous grin. "You rock stars are all the same," she teased.

"My rock star days are over," he said and she was pleased to see that he'd returned to his lighthearted nature.

"Oh?"

"I thought all I needed was the stardom. Turns out the love I was looking for, in the music, in the rush of performing—it isn't there. That's why I could never find it. Why I was never happy. It's in you, Ruby. I love you."

She smiled. "I love you, Mitch Adams. Only you. Always."

THANKS SO MUCH FOR READING! Be sure to check out the entire Wild Irish series.

Come Monday

Ruby Tuesday

Waiting for Wednesday
Sweet Thursday
Friday I'm in Love
Saturday Night Special
Any Given Sunday
Wild Irish Christmas

AND DON'T MISS the next generation, Wilder Irish.
Wild Passion
Wild Desire
Wild Devotion
Wild at Heart
Wild Temptation
Wild Kisses
Wild Fire
Wild Spirit
Wild Side
Wild Night
Wild Embrace
Wild Dreams
Wild Chance

FANS OF WILD Irish AND Facebook! There's a group for you. Come join the Wild Irish Facebook group for sneak peaks, cover reveals, contests and more! Join now.

BE sure to join my newsletter for a **FREE** Wilder Irish short story, One Wild Night.

Waiting for Wednesday

Lane used to be hands off and Tris knew it. He followed the rules and left her alone. Now she's back and the game has changed.

When Lane returned, she believed she could resist the far too sexy Tris. A life of disappointment had destroyed her ability to love, to trust a man.

Or so she thought.

Excerpt:

"Lane?" Tristan looked down at the frail form of his best friend lying in the hospital bed and gently took her hand in his.

Her eyelids fluttered and one—the right one—opened slightly. Her left eye was bruised and swollen shut.

"Tris." Her voice was hoarse, drawing his gaze to

her throat where he could see the faint marks left by her abusive husband's fingers.

"I'm right here, kitten. How are you?" He mentally chastised himself for the stupid question. She was a billboard for domestic violence, every inch of her pale, delicate flesh covered with bruises and cuts. In addition to her black eye, she had a split lip and several stitches above her brow. It hurt him just to look at her and he had to swallow back the murderous rage building in his chest.

"Oh, you know," she said. "Pulled a double shift at work. Got a paper cut. Same old shit."

He grimaced at her joke. It was so like her. Damn woman hated anything even resembling pity, but this time he couldn't let her make light of her predicament.

"Dammit, Lane." He dropped down into the chair by the side of her bed. "Don't do that, babe. Don't make a fucking joke of this."

She winced at his words and he instantly regretted them when she closed her good eye against the tears gathering there. It took her several moments to compose herself enough to speak again. "I'm sorry."

"Don't be sorry, Lane. Just tell me what happened."

"I took your advice. Got up the nerve to leave. Apparently James wanted me around more than he let on."

Tristan tightened his grip on her hand, trying to hide the fact his was trembling in the face of what she'd gone through. Her husband had always been distant, cruel in an emotionally abusive way, according to Lane. As she'd said once, she'd been miserable in her marriage since "about five minutes after the vows". That's when James had started criticizing every aspect of her personality, her looks, her housekeeping. She'd spent two years living in wedded hell with the man.

"I didn't know he would…" he started, guilt crushing him. He'd been encouraging her to leave James for weeks. Trying to convince her she didn't have to spend the rest of her life paying for one mistake. She'd simply fallen in love with the wrong man. With that love gone, he'd assured her there was no shame in admitting defeat and moving on.

"Oh no, Tris," she said, squeezing his hand. "I'm not blaming you. Leaving was…" She paused for a moment. "Leaving *is* the right thing to do. I was a fool for not realizing how angry James would be, but I swear to you, he's never lifted a finger to hurt me. Not once in these past two years."

Tris nodded, wanting her to know he believed her. She may have stayed in an unhappy marriage because of her sense of responsibility, but she would never have remained in a dangerous home. "I know that."

"I honestly, foolishly, thought he didn't give a damn about me."

Tris wanted to reassure her that thought was correct. No man would hurt his wife like this if he gave even the tiniest shit about her. Again, his temper spiked and he suspected if James wasn't already in police custody, Tristan's next trip would have ensured Lane's husband would need similar medical care. Still, he worried about what her words meant.

"You can't go back there, Lane. You can't go back to that marriage."

"I'm not," she added quickly. "There's no way in hell. I just wanted you to know that while I was unhappy the last couple of years, I wasn't a battered wife or anything."

He took a deep breath and fought the urge to disagree with her. James Bryce may not have hit his wife, but his words had beaten down and chiseled away her confidence for years. Saying so, however, would upset her, and he refused to add to the pain she was suffering.

"I know that." If he'd ever once seen a bruise on her, he would have dragged her out of her home and away from the asshole she called a husband. "I was worried when you didn't show up tonight," he said.

Every Wednesday night after her nursing shift, Lane came into his family's restaurant, Pat's Irish Pub, where he was the bartender. She'd plop down at the end of the bar and they'd talk for hours while he served drinks and she sipped her white wine.

Originally, they'd talked about politics, sports, music, movies. For months they had chatted as acquaintances until at some point—Tris had no idea when, exactly—the relationship had evolved into a genuine friendship and the conversations had become much more personal. They'd talked about their child-hoods and dreams for the future. He'd known from the first she was married and he'd respected that. Despite a reputation—according to his sisters—as a ladies' man, he never hit on married women.

Lane was the only woman to ever test his resolve on that unwritten edict. He simply couldn't resist the allure of standing—and yes, flirting—week after week across the counter of the bar from her. She was funny and sweet, smart and sexy. She drew him like a moth to a flame and somewhere along the line, she'd become his best friend.

"I thought Wednesday would be the best night to leave. It's James' late night at the store."

He nodded. One of the reasons why Lane came to the pub Wednesdays was because her husband worked the late shift at a local business, not returning home until after midnight. He glanced at his watch. It was only a little past one in the morning. Too early for James to have wrought so much damage. "So what happened?"

"He came home early. Said he had a headache, but I think perhaps he suspected my plans. I don't know."

"You should have called me. I would have helped you pack up. Helped you leave." Even as he spoke the words, he knew she would never have asked for help. She possessed more than her share of independence. Lane Bryce was determined to be a woman who took care of herself. Her childhood had molded that trait, set it in concrete, and he knew it was hard for her to depend on anyone.

She sighed heavily and he could see how much their conversation was zapping her remaining energy. "Are you in pain?" he asked. "I can call for the nurse."

"She already gave me something. I think it's kicking in."

He'd called her cell phone several times when she'd failed to show up at the pub. A gut feeling he couldn't explain had told him something was wrong. She'd never missed a Wednesday. Not once in almost a year and a half. She'd confessed once to waiting for Wednesday the way some kids waited for their birthday—with anticipation, excitement.

An hour earlier, she'd finally called and told him she was in the hospital. He'd told Ewan to take over the bar and he'd driven through the city, breaking every damn speed limit to reach her.

"I'm just so tired," she said.

"I'm here now," he said as she appeared to drift off to sleep.

"I knew you'd be worried," she mumbled. "I don't know what to do now."

And it was that softly spoken admission that broke what small part of his heart hadn't shattered upon first seeing her so battered in the bed.

"You don't have to do anything, kitten. I'm here now. I'll take care of everything. I'll take care of *you*. I promise."

He was confused when her gaze refocused on him and he sensed her quiet tension. Then she nodded and he breathed a sigh of relief. Accepting help didn't come easily to her, but she had to know, had to realize there was nothing he wouldn't do for her.

"I'm going to go to sleep," she said. "Why don't you go on home for now?"

He shook his head, but she cut off his refusal.

"There's no way you'll fit on that tiny couch, Everest." She'd jokingly begun referring to him by the pet name several months ago. He topped her by at least half a foot and a hundred pounds. "Go home and get some rest. James is in jail and I'll still be here tomorrow."

It was those words that reverberated in his mind when he looked at the empty hospital bed Thursday morning. She wasn't there. She was gone.

Gone.

Waiting for Wednesday is available now.

About the Author

Virginia native Mari Carr is a New York Times and USA TODAY bestseller of contemporary romance novels. With over two million copies of her books sold, Mari was the winner of the Romance Writers of America's Passionate Plume award for her novella, Erotic Research. She has over a hundred published works, including her popular Wild Irish and Compass books, along with the Trinity Masters series she writes with Lila Dubois.

Follow Mari:
www.maricarr.com
mari@maricarr.com